# DINO MIKE

A Novel by
**Jason Singleton**

Illustrations by
Sophie Mitchell

PRESS

TEXT COPYRIGHT © 2023 BY JASON SINGLETON

ILLUSTRATIONS COPYRIGHT © 2023 BY SOPHIE MITCHELL

ALL RIGHTS RESERVED. THIS IS A WORK OF FICTION FROM THE AUTHOR'S IMAGINATION.

FIRST PUBLISHED IN THE UNITED STATES BY 1 TON PRESS LLC IN 2023.

LIBRARY OF CONGRESS CONTROL NUMBER: 2020905808

ISBN 978-1-7346162-0-0 (PAPERBACK)

ISBN 978-1-7346162-1-7 (EBOOK)

ISBN 978-1-7346162-2-4 (AUDIOBOOK)

THE TEXT IN THIS BOOK IS SET IN MRS EAVES OT

ASIDE FROM REVIEWS, NO PART OF THIS PUBLICATION MAY BE REPRODUCED, STORED, OR TRANSMITTED IN ANY FORM OR BY ANY MEANS WITHOUT WRITTEN PERMISSION FROM THE PUBLISHER. CONTACT INFO@1TON.PRESS FOR MORE INFORMATION.

1 TON PRESS LLC

LAS VEGAS, NV

WWW.1TON.PRESS

For Taela

CHAPTER ONE
# THE GOOD LANDS

Dino Mike peered through the branches of a firethorn bush, and his stomach brayed like a battered donkey. A Troodon at the bottom of the hill stopped preening her feathers and perked her head up. Dino Mike held his breath and ducked out of sight. The Troodon went about her business.

Another bush rustled. The Troodon flicked out the retractable claws on her toes and hissed. Delilah Credacious, a deinonychus like Dino Mike, limped into view.

"Oh, thank goodness," Delilah said. Her feathers were as frazzled as her tone. "Darling, I need help. Please, will you help me?"

The Troodon lowered her guard, if only slightly. "What's the matter?"

"I think I . . ." Delilah started. "Oh!" She tumbled to the ground.

The Troodon hurried over. "Are you okay?"

"I'm not sure," said Delilah. "I think it might be broken."

"Lie still," the Troodon said. "I'll call for help." She cocked her head back.

"No, wait," said Delilah. "I mean, *shh*. What if it hears you?"

"What if what hears me?"

"The, uh, allosaurus."

"I've never seen an allosaurus in the Good Lands."

"Me neither," said Delilah. "But I wasn't running from nothing."

"I don't know what you were running from, honey," the Troodon said. "But unless the sauropods came back from migration early and started eating meat, there's nothing big enough here to bother you or me. Are you sure you didn't hit your head?"

"No," said Delilah. "I don't even remember how I got here."

Dino Mike basked in Delilah's performance, his body camouflaged by the firethorn's blue foliage and orange berries. Behind him, someone cleared their throat. Odin Nightcuss tapped his foot in the brush.

"Right," Dino Mike said. "Don't mess up." He drew a breath and crawled out of the bush.

"Agh!" Delilah yelled. She winced and grabbed her ankle.

"Let me take a peek," said the Troodon, looking the foot over. "There's not much swelling. Maybe you just sprained it? Let me get something to wrap it with."

"No, wait," said Delilah. She grabbed the Troodon's wrist. The Troodon knocked her away. Delilah shrunk. "I'm sorry," she said. "I just wanted to see if you could help me up. Maybe I can walk it off?"

The Troodon huffed, and her eyes softened. She reached down. "I'm sorry," she said. "That's not me, honey. Eggsitting will drive anyone bonkers."

Delilah smiled and took her hand. Behind them, Dino Mike crept toward the Troodon's unguarded nest.

Dino Mike exhaled and looked down. Three eggs stared back. Three large, round, succulent, glorious, mouthwatering eggs. Dino Mike wiped away a glob of saliva and wriggled his digits. He picked up an egg, and his stomach growled like a dying iguanodon. The Troodon snapped around and hissed. Dino Mike dropped the egg. The color drained from his face.

"What are you doing, doofus?" Delilah said. "Get the eggs!"

The Troodon slashed at Delilah.

"The eggs!" Delilah repeated. She shuffled, dodged, and ran the other way.

Dino Mike gathered the eggs and bolted. The Troodon barked and darted after him.

One thing nobody could take away from Dino Mike was his speed. He was a world-class sprinter, and thanks to his intricate frame and exceptional agility, he could weave and wiggle his way through passages so dangerous no dinosaur would dare follow, even if they could manage to keep up. He'd never been chased by a Troodon, however, and this mother's persistence was making him nervous. She might not have been able to match his top speed, but he wasn't losing her by any stretch, and stamina was not one of his strong suits.

Even as the Troodon kept pace, she continued to bark out calls for help between angry hisses. More nerve-racking to Dino Mike were the calls he heard back. They were not alone.

Dino Mike shifted directions. He leapt over a fallen tree and ducked under another. The Troodon matched his maneuver without breaking stride. Dino Mike worried about what would happen if she were to catch up. Maybe they could talk it out. Maybe he could get her to see his side of the equation. Maybe—

*SMACK!* Another Troodon jumped out from behind a tree, and Dino Mike barreled into him. The eggs flew skyward. Dino Mike and the Troodon crashed to the ground. A leafy plant caught the eggs and broke their fall. One of them rolled within an inch of Dino Mike's snout. It didn't sit there long before its mother snatched it up.

Dino Mike lifted his head in a daze. The Troodon mother probably could have pummeled him herself, but that wasn't going to be necessary. The male Troodon that Dino Mike knocked over climbed to his feet. Another walked up to join the party. He was much larger than the first two, and his hands were balled into fists.

"Can we talk about this?" Dino Mike said.

The Troodon mother hissed. Dino Mike gulped. The males closed in. Dino Mike buried his head and braced for a beating.

"What's going on here?" came a gruff voice Dino Mike couldn't have been happier to hear. Odin Nightcuss buried the Troodons in his shadow. They took a collective step back.

Dino Mike got to his feet and dusted himself off.

"Well?" Odin said.

The Troodon mother cradled her unhatched children. The larger male stepped in front of her and spoke. "If you came for the eggs, we have a problem."

"I don't know what you're talking about," Odin said. He gave no indication of having been in on the ploy. "What is the situation with the boy?"

"That scumbag tried to steal my babies," said the mother. "And his ratty-tat girlfriend was in on it."

"Hey, she's not my girlfriend," Dino Mike argued.

"Is she in your pack?" the larger male asked.

"I don't know who you're talking about," said Odin.

"Of course not," the larger male said.

"He's protecting her," said the mother.

"I'll handle this," said the male. He made Dino Mike's knees feel like rubber. "Where's your girlfriend?"

"He doesn't have a girlfriend," Odin said. "He doesn't even talk to girls. He's scared to."

The smaller Troodon sniggered. Dino Mike squirmed.

"He stole your eggs?" Odin said.

"He tried to," said the mother.

"I'm sorry to hear that," said Odin. "Do what you have to do. I understand."

Dino Mike's blood froze. Had he heard Odin right?

The Troodons exchanged glances. The mother ran a claw over her throat.

"Are the eggs okay?" the larger male asked.

The mother nodded and kissed her eggs. Dino Mike wilted with shame.

"I think we're done here," the larger male said. He aimed a claw at Dino Mike. "I don't have to tell you what happens if I see you again."

The Troodon mother hissed and departed. The Troodon males followed her into the jungle. Dino Mike slowed his breathing. His heart rate returned to normal, but he was helpless to stop shaking. He was alive, thanks entirely to Odin, but like he always managed to do, he'd mucked everything up. Because of him, the pack would go hungry. Again. When he finally worked up the courage to look Odin in the eye, Odin refused to meet his stare. Instead, Odin turned and walked away.

CHAPTER TWO
# CLEVER GIRL

Maybe it was just Dino Mike, but the jungle seemed more destitute than normal on the way home. Odin and the others hadn't bothered to wait up, and quite frankly, he didn't blame them. He wouldn't have waited for himself either. It wasn't like he was in a hurry to get home. He was about as anxious to see the pack as they were to see him.

Odin's words played on repeat in Dino Mike's head. *Do what you have to do. I understand.* Did Odin really mean it? He shivered, recalling the iciness in Odin's stare.

Dino Mike crouched next to the remains of an unfortunate Herbie that must have been lying there for months. Oddly enough, he found the skeleton relatable, not because his bones were equally as bare, but because he knew how it felt to have the whole world against you. He wondered how long it would take the pack to notice if he didn't come back at all. They probably wouldn't, he concluded. Even if they did, they wouldn't care, no one but Betty. Betty would be devastated, though, and for a moment, this weighed heavily on Dino Mike's mind. She'd get over it, he decided. Betty had a life of her own. She had the great and mighty Odin Nightcuss all to herself, not to mention everything else they had to look forward to.

A slimy sensation crawled over Dino Mike's foot. He launched like a bottle rocket and kicked his leg in midair. A plantain-size centipede plopped on the ground.

"Gross," Dino Mike said, but his stomach begged to differ. It rumbled, reminding him how hungry he was.

The centipede's antennae twitched. Dino Mike's body eclipsed the setting sun.

Dino Mike swallowed and burped. A hundred-legged smile crawled across his face. He glanced down at his new Herbie friend. The skeleton stared blankly.

"You should have said something if you were hungry," Dino Mike said. Not surprisingly, he got no reply.

Feeling better with something in his belly, Dino Mike realized how silly his previous notion was. He bid the skeleton farewell and chucked aside the thoughts he had about running away.

Far ahead, Odin and Delilah were still seething about the situation at hand. Shank Nightcuss, Odin's brother, slashed a tall-bladed plant.

"He has to go, or I'll get rid of him myself," Shank said.

"What do you want me to do?" said Odin. "The kid is Betty's little brother."

"It doesn't matter," said Shank. "You have to do what's right for the pack."

"He's as much a member of it as you are," said Odin.

They stopped at the base of a small waterfall. Delilah's eyes lit up. She waded in the pool and pursed her lips for a long, cold drink. Shank didn't take his eyes off Odin.

"You know what's funny?" Shank said. "I hear your voice, but I don't hear what *you* have to say."

Odin growled. "What's that supposed to mean?"

"It means if you're the one in charge, why don't you act like it?"

Odin flicked his claws like switchblades. Shank did the same. They squared off, ready to shred each other. Delilah pulled up a boulder to watch.

"If you have a problem with the way I run this pack, now would be the appropriate time to say something," Odin said.

Shank could only snarl. He couldn't take Odin, and they both knew it. Delilah, disappointed in Shank's silence, stood up.

"I don't know what you see in her in the first place," Delilah said. "You could do better."

"What's that supposed to mean?" Shank snapped.

"Nothing," said Delilah. "It's just my opinion."

"Who said you had one?" said Shank. He sheathed his claws and stormed off.

Delilah grinned. Odin lowered his weapons and chuckled.

\* \* \*

Heterodontosauridae were peculiar creatures as it were, but one particular Heterodontosaurus who crept through the jungle couldn't have looked more out of place. It wasn't his beak or the awkward tusks protruding from it, and it had nothing to do with the plots of porcupine quills quivering down his back. It was his presence in the Good Lands that was the most peculiar thing about this particular Heterodontosaurus. After all, Heterodontosauridae were Herbies.

The Heterodontosaurus appeared to be alone. All he could hear, aside from the faint pattering of his own footsteps, were the sounds of crickets and running water. When he noticed he was leaving behind a distinct trail of prints, he used a branch like a broom to sweep them away. Satisfied, he tossed his broom aside and took a step. Something crunched under his foot.

The Heterodontosaurus lifted his leg. A tiny twig lay broken in two. The Heterodontosaurus scanned his surroundings. The crickets, who had stopped chirping, started again, and the Heterodontosaurus's spirit practically leapt from his body. He landed on solid ground and checked his pulse. He didn't notice the bush shaking behind him.

The Heterodontosaurus came to a river and tiptoed along the water. Bushes shook in succession behind him, stopping when he glanced over his shoulder. The Heterodontosaurus's eyes narrowed with suspicion. He increased his pace and raced the running water. The rippling bushes kept up with ease. At his wit's end, the Heterodontosaurus pumped his brakes and jump-spun around. The bushes held stationary.

Something snapped distantly. The Heterodontosaurus turned. This time, it wasn't his fault. A bush shook beside him, and a long, terrible head popped out. Bernadette, a feisty velociraptor, grinned. She was close enough to kiss him.

"Clever girl," the Heterodontosaurus said. Before he could run, Bernadette pounced.

In a plume of dust and feathers, the two rolled around in the dirt. They hit a bump, and Bernadette flew off mid-tumble. The Heterodontosaurus hopped up but quickly wished he hadn't. Bernadette's brothers, Hack and Shrapnel, had him flanked on either side.

"Everything okay, Bernie?" Hack asked.

Bernadette stood and smiled. The Heterodontosaurus smiled back. Hack and Shrapnel smiled too. It was bizarre, like a platypus about to be mugged by three happy chickens. The Heterodontosaurus puffed his chest and hissed. The velociraptors laughed like jackals.

Feathers flew like in a pillow fight. Amid snips and snarls, the scratched-up Heterodontosaurus squirted from the pile and scampered down the river. The raptors clambered after him.

"Pull over," Shrapnel said.

The Heterodontosaurus knew better. He wasn't getting off with a ticket.

Hack reared up for a collision. The Heterodontosaurus ducked and covered his head. Hack sideswiped and flew over the top of him, taking out Shrapnel. Bernadette tumbled headfirst over the Heterodontosaurus's back, narrowly avoiding his quills.

The Heterodontosaurus popped up and weighed his options. On one side, the river turned to a raging waterfall. On the other, the raptors groaned and got to their feet. They stood between him and the only path that didn't involve jumping off a cliff. The waterfall, the Heterodontosaurus decided, had far fewer teeth. He plugged his nose and jumped, landing with a splash a mere ten feet below. It was the same waterfall where Delilah had stopped for a drink.

Bernadette whistled. The Heterodontosaurus spun around. Hack and Shrapnel landed with two thuds at Bernadette's side. The Heterodontosaurus had nowhere to go.

"What's going on here?" came a voice nobody recognized. The raptors and Heterodontosaurus turned. It was Dino Mike.

"Nothing," Hack said. "Mind your business."

"Mind your manners," said Dino Mike. He took a step forward, but his shadow didn't do him any favors. "What is the situation with the Herbie?"

Seizing a glimmer of hope, the Heterodontosaurus slunk off to the side. Shrapnel spotted him immediately.

"Where do you think you're going?"

"Just stretching my legs," said the Heterodontosaurus.

"Well?" said Dino Mike.

"Well what?" said Bernadette. "We're hungry. You got a problem with that?"

Dino Mike looked at the Heterodontosaurus. He was cold, wet, and trembling. He didn't deserve what was going to happen to him, and three against one didn't seem fair.

"As a matter of fact, I do," Dino Mike said. "I'm bigger. And I'm hungrier."

The raptors exchanged looks. They were smaller than Dino Mike, sure, but they were nowhere near as scraggy.

"Tough turkey," Hack said. "We saw him first."

"I'm not sure you understand how the food chain works," said Dino Mike.

"I'm not sure you know how to count," said Hack.

Hack was right. Dino Mike was not a fighter, and three raptors could have likely taken him with ease. Still, when Dino Mike looked down at the shivering Heterodontosaurus, the only thing he couldn't do was nothing. He unfolded his dull, clunky claws.

"I forgot that velociraptors were the only Carnies who hunted in packs," Dino Mike said.

"He's bluffing," said Shrapnel.

"Am I?" said Mike.

Shrapnel looked to his sides for support, but Hack and Bernie had taken a step back. Dino Mike cocked his head and barked. The raptors spazzed at the knees.

"On second thought, just let us know if there're any leftovers, m'kay?" Bernadette said. She clonked into Hack, who knocked into Shrapnel, and the three of them scurried away.

Dino Mike let out a breath. It was a good thing the raptors had bought it. No one had responded to his call.

"You should go. It's not safe for you here," Dino Mike said. He didn't get a reply. The Heterodontosaurus was already gone.

Dino Mike shrugged. He was about to head home himself when he noticed something floating in the water. It looked like any other leaf at first, but leaves weren't normally folded and creased. Dino Mike picked it up and opened it, and his mouth fell open. Either the Heterodontosaurus had stolen a toddler's drawing, or the leaf was some sort of map.

CHAPTER THREE
# ALPHA BETTY

Betty Deinonychus-Nightcuss straightened her stiff neck, but her fake smile could not mask her utter lack of sleep.

"How did it go?" Betty said. Odin squatted with a blank stare. "Not again, Odin."

"It's not our fault," said Odin. "There's nothing out there."

"So the Herbies went extinct overnight?" said Betty.

"He's telling the truth," said Delilah. She shook out her feathers. "It wasn't our fault. It was that dimwit brother of yours."

Betty squinted and squashed Delilah in her mind. "Where's Shank?" Betty asked.

"Upset," said Odin.

"At what?" said Betty.

"The usual," Delilah said. "Michael Deinonychus cost us a meal."

Betty gritted her teeth. "Do you mind?"

"Not at all," said Delilah.

Odin motioned his head. "Beat it."

"Fine," Delilah said. She smiled and strutted away.

Betty glared at Odin. "What is she talking about? And where is Michael?"

"We stumbled across some eggs on the way home," Odin said. "Michael messed everything up."

"I thought you said there was nothing out there?"

"There wasn't. We were literally on our way back when we found them."

"And?"

"And I had Delilah run interference while Shank and I secured the perimeter. It was a simple plan. All Michael had to do was grab the eggs, but he couldn't manage that."

"What perimeter?" Betty said. "What were you running interference on?"

Odin hesitated. "The nest was . . . protected."

"Why were you messing with the eggs if there was a Herbie there?"

"It wasn't a Herbie."

"What was it? A bird? A croc?"

"It wasn't one of those either."

Betty's forehead wrinkled. She covered her mouth when she realized what Odin wasn't saying. "Oh, no, you didn't," Betty said. "Please tell me you didn't."

"It was a Troodon, Betty."

"Troodons are Carnies!" Betty said. She swatted at Odin like he was covered in flies. "How could you?"

Odin shielded his face. "We weren't going to eat the Troodon. We were going to eat the eggs. I haven't eaten in eight days."

"I don't care if it's been eight weeks," said Betty. "We don't eat our own kind, let alone their unborn children."

"Well, we didn't, because your brother can't do anything right, so . . ."

"I'm not going to sit here and let you pawn your poor judgment off on him."

"It's my job to do what's right for the pack," Odin said. "It's not just his hunting. The kid is awkward and clumsy. He doesn't fit in. Shank thinks I should kick him out of the pack, and I'm considering it. I'm done going hungry because of him."

"You would leave my brother alone to fend for himself?"

"Your brother. Not mine."

Betty's blood braised her vessels. Her eyes shifted, and her heart sank. "Michael."

Odin squeezed his temples.

"Hey, Betty," Dino Mike said. He snuck past Odin and slouched to kiss Betty's cheek. "How are the eggos?"

"They're great, Michael. I'm glad somebody cares enough to ask."

Betty grabbed Dino Mike's arm and pulled herself up. A pad of vegetation lay beneath her. Two spotted eggs were stuck in the muck. Dino Mike's tummy grumbled quietly, but he was probably the only one who noticed.

"Michael, we need to talk," Odin said.

"Really?" said Betty. "I think you've said enough already."

"This is my decision to make," said Odin. "Not yours."

"I suggest you sleep on it, then," said Betty. "Because your actions come with consequences, like everyone else's."

Odin fumed.

"Why don't you get some rest, Michael?" Betty said. "It's been a long day."

Dino Mike nodded. He hugged Betty and tiptoed past Odin, accidentally crossing Delilah's line of sight. Delilah gave Mike the coldest of shoulders. Dino Mike withered and slithered away.

Odin sighed heavily. "Can we talk about this?"

"No," Betty said, raking leaves over her eggs. "And I don't want to look at you, either."

Odin snorted.

In the loneliest corner of the den, Dino Mike fell onto a plush bed of leaves. A wild bush with juicy, red berries served as his headboard. A glow-in-the-dark infinity twinkled in the sky. Dino Mike took to cataloguing the stars, noting how some stood out in terms of boldness or brilliance. Many of them were average, most even. Some flickered with dull insignificance. Some stars congregated, forming complex designs several times more intriguing than the individuals ever could have been themselves. Others were left out in the cold, surrounded by darkness.

One cluster of stars grabbed Dino Mike's attention and refused to let go. He felt like he'd seen it before, but it wasn't a night sky he was recalling. Dino Mike unfolded the Heterodontosaurus's map. Two words were scrawled at the top, though a few of their letters had been formed backward. Seven dots accompanied them. The words? *Follow Poseidon.* The dots? Arranged exactly like the cluster.

"What are you doing?" Odin said.

Dino Mike dropped the map. "Nothing," he lied.

"You better stay doing nothing," said Odin. "I'll see you in the morning."

Odin left. Dino Mike sank deeper in his bed of leaves. He was getting kicked out of the pack, he just knew it. He needed something to keep his mind busy.

Dino Mike dug the map out for a closer look. Beneath the dots and words were three symbols: a blob, a pile of bones, and a tree. A faint line squiggled down from the tree to a circle. At the bottom, two oversized *m*'s (or were they zigzags?) spanned the width of the leaf.

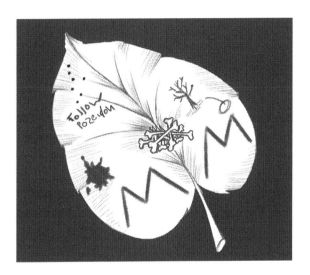

*Follow Poseidon.*

The words confused Dino Mike a little more each time he read them. His eyes grew heavy as he contemplated their meaning.

\* \* \*

With great velocity, a short, highly sharpened stick stuck in the mud at Shank Nightcuss's feet. From his seat on a stump, Shank snatched a new branch and whittled it furiously.

Something crunched. Shank slung his new weapon over his shoulder. It sank in the bark of a tree inches from Odin's face. Addled, Odin grabbed the stick and tried to wriggle it free. It wouldn't budge, and the back end broke off in his hand.

"Is this what you do with your free time?" Odin asked. He waved the broken stick.

"Step in front of the next one if you want to see how I feel," said Shank.

Odin tossed the stick aside and took a seat on an empty stump. He pulled a finished spear out of the mud and turned it over.

"You know, you could do some real damage with these," Odin said.

"That would be the idea," said Shank.

"What if you made it longer?" Odin asked. "To account for larger prey."

"What prey?" Shank spat. He knocked Odin's spear aside and tore another branch from his tree, this one twice as big. "There is no prey."

Odin sighed.

"What is it?" Shank said. "Betty?"

Odin nodded.

"Is she ever not mad at you?"

"Doesn't seem like it," said Odin. Shank laughed. Odin cleared his throat. "I spoke with her about Michael. I told her I was thinking about sending him packing."

Shank stopped mid-shear. "What did she say?"

"That she loved me. Then she kissed me good night."

"Right." Shank finished his cut, brought the tip of the spear to his mouth, and blew off the debris. His eyes fixated on the point. "What happens next?"

"I don't know, Shank. I really don't."

Odin was on the verge of breaking down. Shank lowered his spear and softened his tone. "Relax," Shank said. "Don't let her rumple your feathers. You have to do what's right for the pack, and she should have your back on that."

"It's her brother, Brother."

"I wouldn't care if it were her father, Brother," said Shank. "It's a jungle out there. Only the strong survive. What happens when those eggs hatch? Are you going to let your kids starve for Michael Deinonychus's sake?"

If Shank's intent was to comfort Odin, his kick sailed wide. Odin pinched his shoulder. "I can't do it," Odin said. "I'd be a terrible dad. Why can't we just eat our young like they did in the old days?"

Shank flashed a rare smile. "Scared much?"

"Petrified."

"Good. At least you're scared of something."

"What are you scared of?" Odin asked.

"Nothing," Shank said. "That's the problem."

A twig snapped. Delilah froze like a popsicle.

"What are you doing here?" Shank asked.

"Nothing," Delilah said.

"Are you spying on us?"

"No. Geez, I was just—"

"Just what?" said Shank. "Don't geez me. Spit it out."

"I was just going to bed," Delilah said. "I wanted to see how long you were going to be."

"As long as I take," said Shank. "Mind your own business."

"I thought you were my business," said Delilah.

"There you go thinking again," said Shank. "We're talking here. Scram."

Delilah's nose tingled. Odin mocked Shank behind his back. Delilah smirked. Shank spun. Odin turned Shank's newer, longer spear over and pretended nothing happened.

"Better," Odin said. "But wouldn't it be twice as effective if you sharpened both ends?"

Shank growled. A vein pulsed in his forehead.

\* \* \*

Dino Mike's snores cycled from muffled to clamorous and back again. He'd fallen asleep with the map on his face, and it fluttered with every breath he took. Delilah stormed out of the woods and stumbled over him. Her face was sticky with tears.

"Oof!" Dino Mike grunted. He hunched over. Delilah fretted at his side. "What happened?" Dino Mike asked. "Are you all right?"

"No, I'm not," Delilah said. "You tripped me, you oaf."

"I didn't mean to," said Dino Mike. "I must have sleep-tripped you."

"Maybe you should sleep somewhere else."

"I sleep here every night. This is my bed."

"Whatever. I'm not arguing," Delilah said. She pulled her knees to her chest and buried her head. "Just leave me alone, all right?"

Something had to have happened, Dino Mike thought. She couldn't have been that upset at him. He offered her a leaf to wipe her nose.

"Get that away from me," Delilah said.

"I'm just trying to help," said Dino Mike.

"Your help is the last thing I need."

"That may be true. But you do have boogers running down your face."

Delilah snatched the leaf, blew her nose like a foghorn, and handed it back. Only then did Dino Mike notice he'd given her his map. Delilah looked marginally better, so he wasn't offended. Discreetly, he wiped gobs of her mucus off in the dirt.

"Do you want to tell me what really happened?" Dino Mike asked.

"I already did," Delilah said. "If you don't leave me alone, I'm going to tell Shank."

Dino Mike lowered his head. Shank was the last dinosaur he wanted to see, especially with Odin upset at him. Still, he couldn't bear to see Delilah in the state she was in, and he suspected Shank was at fault.

"Did Shank do something?" Dino Mike asked. Delilah didn't answer. "Do you want me to say something to him?"

"Actually, I want you to mind your own business," Delilah said. She tried to come off harsh, but Dino Mike could tell she was flattered by his foolish suggestion.

"I'm not scared of him," Dino Mike said. "I mean, I am. Terrified, actually. But if something happened I—"

"It's not that serious," Delilah said. She twirled a feather. "He's just so into himself. It's like, every time he does or says something nice, he has to do or say something nasty to make up for it."

Dino Mike couldn't believe it. Delilah was opening up. There was a bona fide crack in the door. He scooched closer.

"What are you doing?" Delilah said. She scooted away.

"Nothing. I mean, I was just trying to comfort you."

"Ew. Bring me food if you want to comfort me. I'm starving because of you."

"That seems to be the consensus," Dino Mike said.

"What's that supposed to mean?" said Delilah.

"Nothing," said Dino Mike. "It's not like any of you care anyway." He slid back over, fluffed a pillow, and gazed at the sky.

Delilah fidgeted. "What are you looking at?" she said.

Dino Mike pointed to a dimly lit star isolated from all the rest. "Do you think that star did something wrong?"

"What do you mean?" Delilah said. She yawned.

"Do you think it likes being lonely, or do the other stars have a problem with it?"

"Maybe. Or maybe it just likes being different."

"Maybe," said Dino Mike. He considered telling Delilah about the map. By the time he talked himself into it, though, she was already snoring loudly.

Dino Mike yawned and took one last look at the sky. Maybe it was just him, but the lonely star seemed to flicker a bit brighter than before. Dino Mike shucked a berry from his headboard and plucked a quill from his own stock. He inked the feather with bright red juice from the berry and dabbed the map where he felt the lonely star belonged, not separate from the others, but a part of the group. Satisfied, he tucked the map away and allowed his eyes to shut.

* * *

In a flurry of confusion, Dino Mike found himself face-to-face with a snarling Shank Nightcuss. His sense of sound was warped, and he couldn't breathe. Shank had him held up by the throat. Dino Mike couldn't tell if he was dreaming or not.

Shank growled. Delilah screamed, but Dino Mike couldn't see her from where he was hanging. He could barely make Odin's figure out from the farthest corner of his eye.

"Shank, what's going on?" Odin demanded.

"He loses my eggs, and he thinks it's okay to sleep next to my girl?" Shank said.

"That's not what happened," Dino Mike sputtered. Shank held up a long, sharp, double-sided spear. Dino Mike's eyes tripled in size.

"Shank, no!" Delilah cried.

"Shut up," said Shank.

"Put him down," said Odin.

"I intend to," said Shank. He pulled the spear back.

Betty lunged and tackled Shank from out of nowhere. Dino Mike and the spear fell to the ground. Shank tried to get up, but Betty pressed her foot on his neck.

"Betty," Odin said.

Betty didn't have time to respond. Delilah flicked out her claws, and Betty hissed. Delilah kept her distance. Betty was far fiercer than Delilah was, far fiercer than they all were.

"Are you just going to sit there, Brother?" Shank said.

Odin exhaled. Going against Betty would be an icy, uphill battle. "My hands are tied," said Odin.

"Let's talk about this, Betty. I'm sure it's all one big misunderstanding."

"Allow me to clear it up, then," said Betty. "From here on out, anyone who threatens another member of this pack will be dealt with. Immediately." She pressed her foot down hard enough to shave Shank's feathers. "Is that clear enough for you?"

Shank nodded. He didn't have a choice. No one argued with Betty. Odin might have been their so-called leader, but the pack belonged to her. Betty stepped off Shank's throat and helped Dino Mike up.

"Are you okay?" Betty asked.

"Yeah," Dino Mike said.

"Good," said Betty. "I suggest everyone gets some sleep. Tomorrow's a big day."

CHAPTER FOUR
# EGG DUTY

Dino Mike's wake-up call the next morning wasn't as horrible as it had been the night before, but it wasn't pleasant either. A stone-faced Odin Nightcuss had the pack up before dawn could crack. Even the crickets were still sleeping. Dino Mike wondered if Odin had slept at all.

"Listen up," Odin said. "We're making some changes today."

Betty stood stalwart behind Odin. Delilah rubbed the sleep from her eyes and kept her back to Shank.

"Michael," Odin said. Dino Mike's heart plummeted. A public ousting, how humiliating. "You will not be joining us today," Odin continued.

The words kicked Dino Mike like a mule. He tried to get a read on Betty, but it wasn't possible.

"Betty will be hunting with us instead," Odin added. "You're going to stay back with the eggs. Any questions?"

Delilah turned to Shank before she remembered she was ignoring him. Shank's head looked like it was about to explode. Dino Mike struggled to piece the information together. He hadn't been exiled after all. Instead, he'd been given egg duty.

"Right," Odin said. "We're off. Keep those eggs safe."

Shank was already gone. Delilah wasn't far behind.

"I'll wait for you," Odin whispered to Betty, and he gave her and Mike some privacy.

"Betty, I . . . I . . ." Dino Mike stammered. "I don't know what to say. You're hunting?"

"Yeah," Betty said with a smile. "They could use the help. Don't worry. We'll bring you back some food."

A thousand thoughts fought for relevance on the tip of Dino Mike's tongue. He was only able to verbalize one of them. "Thank you."

"For what?" Betty asked. "Keep my babies safe. I'm counting on you."

* * *

Dino Mike rocked back and forth on top of Betty's eggs. He thought he should do this to keep them warm, but it was uncomfortable to say the least. He had no idea how Betty did it every day, day after day. Maybe that's why she seemed so irritable to the others, in addition to her immense hunger, of course.

When boredom and soreness set in, Dino Mike stood to try something new. Short on ideas, he paced and stroked his chin. What would a cool uncle do? He couldn't take his nieces or nephews anywhere because they weren't allowed to leave. He couldn't feed them anything because eggs don't eat, never mind the food shortage. Dino Mike didn't fancy himself much of a storyteller. They could play a game, he thought. But what? Hide-and-seek? That wouldn't be much fun with eggs. Tag? Same problem.

"I know," Dino Mike said. "We can kick rocks!"

Kicking rocks wasn't only Dino Mike's favorite game to play, but it was also one of the rare things he was actually good at. Even though the eggs couldn't participate, he was content teaching them everything he knew. When the time came, the kids would be naturals.

"First thing you need are rocks," Dino Mike said, rummaging to find the perfect ones. "The rounder, the better." The eggs paid him close attention. "You're also going to need legs. You'll have those soon enough. I'll kick for you for now."

In front of a tree, Dino Mike drew a line in the dirt. Behind it, he placed three exceptionally round rocks. "This is the home tree," he said. He pointed to another in the distance. "That one down there is the mid-tree. What you do is take turns kicking your rocks down and back. Everybody gets a kick, like this."

Dino Mike wound up and kicked the first rock. It was a solid kick, and the rock bounced a decent ways.

"See, that's a good kick. Thing is, it's not always good to go first, because if someone else kicks their rock and it hits yours, they get a choice. They can either kick their rock again, or they can kick your rock in any direction."

Dino Mike slid down the starting line and kicked the second rock. It pelted the first.

"This is where it gets tricky, because if they choose to kick your rock, you can find yourself a long way from your goal."

Dino Mike walked over to the first rock, cocked his leg back, and kicked as hard as he could. The rock sailed deep into the woods, but Dino Mike was too busy hopping on one foot to see where it landed.

"Agh!" Dino Mike yelped. He limped back to the nest. "Anywho, first one to go down, kick their rock off the mid-tree, come back, and kick it off the home tree wins. Questions?"

The eggs had none.

* * *

On the hunting trail, two arguments had broken out.

"I don't know why you're upset," Odin said. "I'm doing the best I can."

"Then do better," said Betty.

"I suppose it's my fault the Herbies left the Good Lands?" said Odin.

"Listen to yourself," said Betty. "How could they leave? Did they swim across the ocean? Or are they eating rocks in the Bad Lands?"

"You're right," Odin said. "They're hiding somewhere, and we're going to find them."

"I'm glad you think this is a joke," said Betty.

Behind them, Delilah's relentless drilling had Shank grinding his teeth. "You had no business eavesdropping on us," Shank said.

"I wasn't," said Delilah. "I was looking for you. You know I hate sleeping alone."

"Is that why I found you lying next to him?"

"Ew. I fell asleep because I was tired," Delilah said. "He must have moved his bed. Why can't you just be happy knowing you have the prettiest dinosaur in the jungle all to yourself?"

"Because she won't leave me alone or shut her trap," said Shank.

"Ugh," Delilah groaned. She launched an elbow. Shank ducked and felt the wind gust over his head.

"It's too bad you can't, you know, lead a pack of your own," Delilah added. She sped to catch up with Betty.

* * *

A round rock sailed through the air and clunked off the home tree.

"Dang," Dino Mike shouted. "You win again. That's five in a row." Dino Mike jogged to the nest, bursting with pride. The eggs looked as happy as he felt. It was the best Dino Mike remembered feeling in a long time.

"I can't wait to play you guys for real. You're going to be really good."

Dino Mike winced. His toe was throbbing and swollen, but he wasn't going to let that put a damper on his day. He gauged the sun, which bore down overhead. It was some time in the afternoon.

"What do you guys want to do now?"

* * *

Odin and Shank lumbered along in silence, enjoying the brief moment of peace only the absence of conversation could provide. The deinonychuses came to the waterfall from the previous day. Betty stopped on a dime.

"What is it?" Delilah asked.

Betty held up a claw. "Shh."

Odin recognized the look on Betty's face. He shifted to a higher state of sensory awareness and joined her at the front of the pack.

"What do you smell?" Odin asked.

"Herbie," Betty said. "I think. It's a little funky."

Shank and Delilah rolled their heads.

"How long?" said Odin.

"A day or less," Betty replied. She scoped the jungle with binocular vision.

"There," said Odin, but Betty was already on top of it. Shank and Delilah unsheathed their claws. Betty hovered over a set of prints that appeared to be brushed over. "I've never seen tracks like those," Odin said.

"Neither have I," Betty admitted.

"I'm down to try something new," said Shank.

Betty stalked the tracks. Odin, Shank, and Delilah backed her up. Betty froze.

"What's wrong?" Odin asked. He looked down. The tracks ended. It was like whatever left them had vanished into thin air. "Maybe someone else got here first?"

"No sign of struggle," Shank said. "Unless it was bite-size, there would be some sort of mess."

"Maybe it flew away," Delilah said.

"That doesn't make any sense," said Betty.

"You said yourself you've never seen tracks like this before," Delilah said. "It's possible is all I'm saying."

"You're right," Betty said. "I'm sorry."

Betty's apology eased the pack's tension. They were all focused on the same thing, and without Michael Deinonychus to slow them down, there was no weak link. A branch crunched nearby. All four of their heads turned. A lonely bush trembled.

Betty nodded. She and Delilah led the way. Odin and Shank flanked them. This was instinctive. This was predatory. The deinonychuses surrounded the bush and pounced. There was growling. There was jaw clamping. The bush went still.

* * *

Dino Mike could not stop shaking. He might have considered it dancing, but if anyone else had been watching, they might have called it having a seizure. Dino Mike didn't care. He was having the time of his life. How could he have noticed the shrub stirring behind the nest?

Whispers inside the bush were too muffled to make out. There was a smack, followed by a harsh whisper, followed by another smack. Two more smacks came next, and three familiar heads popped up. Bernadette winked at Hack and motioned toward Shrapnel with her head. Hack nodded, squatted, and shoved Shrapnel out. Shrapnel rolled to his feet and spun around, but he met the tip of Bernadette's claw, which pressed against his nose and pointed him to the nest. Bernadette disappeared into the shrub. Shrapnel kicked a pebble in after her.

With one eye on Dino Mike and the other on the eggs, Shrapnel tiptoed toward the nest. His arms twitched, and saliva oozed from his mouth. He was eight steps away when Dino Mike spun off rhythm, strumming the air to an off-kilter tune. Shrapnel dove face-first into a bush left of the nest. Dino Mike was none the wiser.

Dino Mike fell into a groove. He hopped from right to left like his body was an oversized spring. Hack's head emerged from a third bush, this one to the nest's right. He extended a wobbly shepherd's crook. Dino Mike pivoted and hopped back. Hack dropped the hook, and it broke into sticks. Dino Mike still didn't notice.

Hack and Shrapnel poked their heads out and argued from opposite sides of the nest. Bernadette's head popped out of the original bush between them.

"Psst," Bernadette whispered. Hack and Shrapnel looked. Bernie touched her nose, her jaw, her nose again, and her ear. Shrapnel and Hack nodded, double-tapped their snouts, and ducked out of sight.

Dino Mike stopped dancing and eyed the bushes suspiciously. Deeming everything kosher, he smiled at the eggs and resumed his shenanigans. He was dangling his forearm from his elbow like a hinge when Bernadette appeared. Dino Mike nearly shot out of his feathers.

"I'm sorry," Bernadette said. "I didn't mean to startle you."

"Pff," Dino Mike said. "I wasn't startled. And, uh, I wasn't dancing either. If that's what you thought."

"I thought it was cute, whatever it was," Bernadette said. She beamed relentlessly. "Do you want to be friends?"

Dino Mike didn't know what to say. He didn't really have any friends, if he was being quite honest. Yet here he was, face-to-face with another living dinosaur who couldn't quit cheesing. How could he say no?

"I, uh, wait a minute," Dino Mike said. "You're that raptor from yesterday."

"Oh yeah," said Bernadette. "That. Did you have any leftovers?"

"Leftover what?"

"Leftover Herbie."

"Oh," Dino Mike said. He tapped his belly, careful not to give himself away. "No, there wasn't much to go around. Sorry."

"It's okay. I get it. I'm Bernadette, but my friends call me Bernie." She offered Dino Mike a hand. "What's your name?"

"Michael Deinonychus," Dino Mike said with a shake. "But, uh, my friends call me Dino Mike." He felt his hand sweating and let go, wondering if he'd squeezed too hard.

Bernadette giggled. "Nice to meet you, Dino Mike."

Dino Mike blushed. No one had ever actually called him that before.

Bernadette spotted the rocks near the home tree. "Do you want to kick rocks or something?"

Dino Mike held his foot up. "Can't. Stubbed my toe."

"Didn't seem to affect your dancing."

"I was trying to keep my mind off it. For the kids, you know. We could play something else, though."

Bernadette looked around. Other than the rocks, there wasn't much to play with. Hack's sticks lay by the nest. "We could rub sticks together."

"Why would we do that?" Dino Mike asked.

"I don't know. Have you ever done it before?"

"No."

"Me neither," said Bernie. "Who says it can't be fun?" Bernadette grabbed the sticks and gave them to Mike.

"You don't want to go first?" Dino Mike asked.

"No, I want to see you try," said Bernadette.

"Okay, fine," said Dino Mike. He took a stick in each hand and rubbed them together. *Fun* was not a word he would have used to describe it.

Bernadette peeked over Dino Mike's shoulder. Hack and Shrapnel peered out of their bushes. Bernadette waved for them to stay low.

"Lower?" Dino Mike said. "What, like, put them down on the ground?"

"Yeah, try that," said Bernie. She held Dino Mike's shoulder, making sure he kept his back to the nest.

Dino Mike jammed one stick to the ground and strummed it with the other. The first kept slipping. "It's not working."

Bernadette scooped some leaves into a small pile. "Here. Use these for traction."

Dino Mike jabbed the leaves. They held the first stick in place, and he was able to rub the other one much faster. "You were right. This is fun," Dino Mike said. "It's like making music."

Bernadette bobbed her head to Dino Mike's imaginary tune and gave a signal behind her back. Hack and Shrapnel sprinted from their bushes. Both scooped an egg up in passing, and they dove into the other's original bush.

"I can't believe I've never done this before," Dino Mike said. "Grab some more sticks, Bernie. We can form a band."

Bernadette's smile lost its luster. "Actually, it's getting pretty late. I have to get going."

"But you just got here," Dino Mike said. "You have to take one turn at least."

Dino Mike forced the sticks into Bernadette's arms, leaving her no choice. "Fine," Bernie said. She strummed the sticks together with vigor, so much so a small trail of smoke formed at their intersection.

"Whoa," Dino Mike said. "What's that?"

"What's what?" said Bernie. A spark jumped and landed on the pile of leaves. They went up in flames. "Uh-oh."

"Ah!" Dino Mike exclaimed.

The blaze spread quickly. It skipped from the leaves to some brush and streaked toward the nest, incinerating it.

"Oh no!" Dino Mike said. "The eggs!"

The flames engulfed the bushes on both sides, ejecting Hack and Shrapnel like hot potatoes. "Ow-wow-yow!" they cried. The eggs rolled. A wall of fire flared up between them.

Dino Mike glanced back at Bernadette. For once, she wasn't smiling.

"You tricked me," Dino Mike said.

"We're hungry," said Bernadette. "Don't take it personal."

Like lightning, Dino Mike bolted. The smoke was thick as wool, making it impossible to see or breathe. All he could hear was the last thing Betty had said to him: *Keep my babies safe. I'm counting on you.*

* * *

Spit swung like a pendulum from Shank's yellow teeth. Odin lugged the remains of a small mammal in front of him. It wasn't much, but it was enough to make Shank lick his chops.

"Why does he get to eat when we're still hungry?" Shank said.

"We operate as a pack, Shank. Not as individuals," said Odin.

Shank snarled. Delilah scratched his back. "If anyone deserves any extra, it's you. You went for the kill."

Shank grumbled lowly. He didn't care what Delilah had to say.

Odin grinned at Betty. "You were amazing today," he said. "As usual."

Betty cracked half a smile. "I thought there wasn't any food out there."

"I can't remember the last time I had mammal," Odin said. "It's almost as good as Herbie, honestly."

Betty's smile faded. Concern washed over her face.

"What did I say?" said Odin.

"Nothing," said Betty. "Do you smell that?"

"Smell what?" said Odin. He coughed.

Betty sprinted around a corner and stopped in her tracks. Clouds of smoke hung in the air where the den used to be. Everything else was ash and rubble. Odin, Shank, and Delilah caught up, and their jaws hit the dirt.

"What happened?" Delilah said.

Betty's eyes zeroed in on a charred black circle. She fell to her knees and clutched her chest. "My eggs!" Betty cried. "My babies!"

"They're here," came a weak, raspy voice. Betty turned. Dino Mike's body could barely be made out against the base of a tree. He was covered in soot, but he cradled Betty's eggs in his arms. "Your babies are safe."

"Michael!" Betty shouted. She embraced him and the eggs.

Odin hoisted Dino Mike by the armpits. Betty licked her finger and wiped Dino Mike's face. "What happened?" Odin asked.

"Raptors," Dino Mike said. "They tried to steal the eggs, and—"

"You burned down our den," Shank snipped.

"Quiet," Odin snapped. "How did the fire start?"

"I don't know," Dino Mike said. "The girl, Bernie, asked if I wanted to kick rocks. I told her no because I stubbed my toe, so she said we should rub sticks together, and we did. But then the sticks started to smoke, and her brothers tried to steal the eggs. I didn't know what was going on, I swear."

"You started a fire by rubbing two sticks together?" said Shank.

"No, she started it," Dino Mike said.

"It happened on your watch," said Shank. "Time's up, Odin. He has to answer for this."

Odin surveyed the ruin. "No, he doesn't."

"What do you mean he doesn't? We don't have a home because of him."

"But our children will," Odin said. Betty smothered her eggs with kisses. "He did what he was supposed to do," Odin went on. "He kept the eggs safe."

Shank unhitched his claws. Odin stepped in front of him, blocking Dino Mike from view. Shank huffed. He put his claws away and calmly took leave. Nobody followed him. They all knew better.

"I'm so glad you're okay," Betty said. She wrapped Dino Mike up and pressed her head against his. The mammal landed with a thud at their feet.

"Go on," said Odin. "You earned it."

"I told you we'd bring you something back," Betty whispered.

Dino Mike salivated, and his tummy rumbled. Through all the commotion, he had forgotten just how hungry he was.

### CHAPTER FIVE
# UNCLE MIKE

*Follow Poseidon.*

The riddle at the top of Dino Mike's map was working his head harder than his brand-new slate pillow. It was nearly morning, but Mike hadn't slept a wink. Hunger pangs aside, he knew Shank had it out for him worse than ever, since he burned down the den. There was no way he was going to let Shank catch him sleeping. Instead, he read the map again and again to distract his restless mind.

The deinonychuses had found a new den, but Dino Mike would've been the first to admit it was a very loose definition of home. The ground was completely flat and consisted of dirt and stone. That was it. It was very level, very basic, and Odin had Betty and the others convinced it was one-hundred-percent fireproof. Nothing even remotely flammable was allowed near the nest, the least of all sticks. Betty insisted her eggs could hatch any day, and Odin wasn't taking any chances.

Odin's new orders had the pack hunting in pairs. Not only did this give them the best chance of finding food since they could hunt around the clock, but it also meant Betty would never be left alone, and the eggs would be safe. Dino Mike didn't mind. He and Odin took the day shift, while Shank and Delilah hunted at night. Dino Mike and Shank didn't even see each other outside of a few uncomfortable moments at shift change. Mike was certain and grateful Odin had taken this into careful consideration.

At the hint of footsteps and angry muttering, Dino Mike tucked his map away and feigned sleep. Shank and Delilah emerged from the woods. Dino Mike kept one eye slit open enough to keep them in his line of sight.

"This is ridiculous," Shank said. He swung a spear. "We're wasting our time out there."

"I'm hungry too," said Delilah. "But fretting isn't going to make the Herbies appear out of nowhere."

"There are no Herbies," said Shank. "There's nothing but Carnies in this jungle."

"What's your point?" said Delilah. Gingerly, she lowered herself onto a rock-hard bed.

"We need to hunt them before they hunt us."

A lump formed in Dino Mike's throat. He fought the urge to swallow it. Delilah swallowed the lump in hers.

"You're just tired," Delilah said. "You don't mean that."

"I don't see any other way," said Shank. "We're all hungry. We're going after each other's eggs. Sooner or later, it's going to come down to us versus them. Why not strike first?"

"Odin and Betty would never go for that," Delilah said. "Come to bed. We can talk about it tomorrow."

Odin and Betty snored. Shank planted his spear like a flag. "We'd have better luck without them," he said with a scowl.

Shank submitted to exhaustion and fell on the slab next to Delilah. He must have landed harder than he'd hoped or forgotten his bed was no longer made of brush, because he shot back up, gripped his elbow in pain, and struggled to hold back every curse word he knew.

"Kah!"

"Are you okay?" Delilah asked.

"Fine," Shank said. He flexed his forearm and lowered himself carefully. A minute later, he was snoring bombastically.

Delilah held her breath. She rolled away from Shank and forced her eyes shut.

Without making a sound, Dino Mike gulped.

* * *

"Are you out of your mind?" Odin yelled. "What were you thinking?"

Dino Mike shot up, realizing he'd dozed off. Everyone else was already alert.

"I haven't slept in three days or had a decent meal in over a week," Shank said. "You'd best get off my back."

"Seriously," Delilah said. "It's no big deal."

"No big deal?" Odin raised Shank's spear. "Sticks start fires. Why would you bring this by the nest?"

"Your idiot brother-in-law starts fires," said Shank. "I think your hunger's gone to your head." He grabbed at the spear, but Odin held it out of reach. "Give it back," Shank said.

"No," said Odin.

Shank tried again. Odin played keep-away.

"I said give it to me," said Shank.

"I can't give you something I can't trust you with," said Odin. Shank tried one more time. Odin shoved Shank backward and hurled the spear into the woods. "There," he said, dusting his hands. "Problem solved."

Shank lunged and slammed Odin to the ground. There, he pivoted on top of him and hooked Odin's arm. "Solve this one," Shank said.

"If you say so," said Odin. He butted Shank's snout with the back of his head. Shank grabbed his bloodied nose. Odin tackled him and put him in a headlock.

Betty walked over with an egg in each arm. "Are you two ever going to grow up?"

"He started it," Odin sputtered.

Betty and Delilah rolled their eyes. "When you're done bonding, do you think you could go find us some food?" Betty said.

"It's no use," Shank choked out. "There's nothing out there."

Betty shook her head. She noticed Dino Mike watching the scuffle, wide-eyed. "Sleep well, Michael?"

Dino Mike shook his head out of a trance. "Huh? Oh, yeah," he lied. "Thanks."

* * *

Dino Mike followed Odin through a dense thicket of trees. They were much taller than the ones where they used to live. The mountains were closer too and much more imposing.

"What are you looking at?" Odin asked. He sported a freshly minted black eye.

"Nothing," Dino Mike said. He looked away.

"It's okay," said Odin. "You should see the other guy."

Dino Mike smiled. He knew Odin had mixed feelings about him, but he genuinely appreciated everything Odin did to help. Then he recalled something, and his smile went away.

"What's up?" Odin said.

"Do you think Carnies are going to start eating each other?" Dino Mike asked.

"Ha!" said Odin. "Why would you ask that?"

"I don't know. I mean, we're going after each other's eggs. What's next?"

Odin chuckled some more. "You're starting to sound like Shank."

Dino Mike didn't laugh. He was afraid to tell Odin that's exactly who he'd heard it from. "But what if they do?" he asked.

"It wouldn't solve anything," said Odin. "There are fewer Carnies in the Good Lands than there ever were Herbies. What would we do when we ran out?"

It was a good point, but Dino Mike didn't think Shank would see it that way. "What if the Herbies don't come back?"

"Are you saying they went somewhere?"

"I don't know. You know what I mean."

"Let me ask you this: How do you think we came to be in the Good Lands in the first place? Or do you think we were always here?"

Dino Mike pondered the question. "I never thought about it, I guess."

"Think about it, then. If you think there's a chance we came from somewhere else, then I think there's a chance there's somewhere else we can go. I mean, the sauropods migrate, right?"

"Yeah, but they're built for travel. Don't they store—"

"That's beside the point," said Odin. "I'm just saying if it's possible there's somewhere else we could go, then it's possible the Herbies could have gone there already. And if they're not coming back, maybe it's time we start thinking about leaving too."

"Leaving the Good Lands?"

Odin silenced Dino Mike with a claw. He tilted his head and sniffed the ground. Dino Mike copied, but he didn't smell anything.

"What is it?" Dino Mike asked.

"I don't know," said Odin. "But it's a little funky." His eyes narrowed, and he plodded headfirst into a field of giant ferns.

Dino Mike followed, but the ferns swayed over his head, and he struggled to keep Odin in sight. Every now and then, he thought he saw Odin's tail bob, but it was hard to say if it really was Odin or just a fern's fronds flapping in the wind.

"Where'd you go?" Dino Mike asked. "What do you smell?" He didn't hear a response. Panic seized his chest.

Dino Mike turned. Nothing but ferns. He spun around. More of the same. Ferns enveloped him, and their invasive green arms prodded him from odd angles.

"Aagghh!" Dino Mike yelled. He picked a direction and ran. Ferns smacked him in the face as he flew. His rib cage grew tight. Something snared his ankle, and his body slammed to the ground.

Dino Mike lifted his head. It was still daytime, but he was seeing stars. He glanced down. A jagged rock stuck up. Dino Mike frowned. He stood, brushed himself off, and went to kick the rock, but something gave him pause. There was a distinct set of footprints next to the rock, and they appeared to be brushed over.

"Michael," Odin said. Dino Mike shrieked and spun. Odin hovered between two ferns.

"Odin," Dino Mike said. "I mean, what?"

"What are you doing?"

"Nothing. I got lost. Did you find anything?"

"No," Odin said. He hesitated. "You all right?"

Dino Mike swallowed. "Yeah," he said. "Tripped over a rock. I'll be fine."

Odin stared Dino Mike down. "Let's go," he said finally. "Try to keep up, will you?"

Dino Mike nodded. Odin disappeared. Not wanting to answer any more questions, Dino Mike kicked some dirt over the tracks.

\* \* \*

By the time Odin and Dino Mike returned home, the sky had turned a deep shade of copper. Betty sat with a warm arm wrapped around Delilah's shoulders. Delilah bawled her eyes out.

"It's okay, honey," Betty said. She patted Delilah and stood. "Odin and Michael are back. You can tell them all about it."

"What's going on?" Odin asked. "What happened?"

"Your brother happened," said Betty.

"Shank? Where is he?" said Odin.

"He left," Delilah said. She tried to hold it together, but she fell into a fit of tears.

"What do you mean left?" said Odin. "Left where?"

Delilah sobbed too hard to piece an answer together. Betty smiled on one side of her face. Only Odin registered the smirk.

"I have to check on the eggs," Betty said. "You got this?"

"Of course," said Odin. He sighed, and Delilah buried her head in his shoulder. Odin glared at Betty behind Delilah's back.

Betty wrung Delilah's tears out of her feathers. "How'd it go, Michael?"

Dino Mike shook his head. "Not well."

"That's okay," said Betty. "Tomorrow's another day."

Later that night, Betty slept on her rock like it was a cloud, but Odin couldn't catch a single z. He wondered how she could even be tired. All she did was sit on eggs all day. He rolled over, trying not to make a big deal out of it.

Dino Mike slept deeply as well. His snores could've scared an allosaurus away. Odin cracked half a smile, but it didn't help his cause. His eyes moved on to their next checkpoint. Delilah's bed lay empty. Odin sat up.

In the woods, Delilah sat on a fallen tree. She wasn't crying, but the moon's light glinted off the mist in her eyes.

"I know you're there," Delilah said.

"How'd you know that?" said Odin.

"Perks of being a predator," said Delilah.

Odin stepped over the horizontal trunk. "Mind if I sit?"

"It's a free jungle."

Odin plopped down and gazed at the sky. "Wow. Would you look at that moon?"

Delilah stared at the dirt. "I don't know if he's coming back, Odin."

"What makes you say that?"

"It's the way he's been talking. He doesn't sound sane."

"Everyone goes through patches," Odin said. "Maybe he just needs some space."

"He wasn't leaving me," Delilah said. "He was leaving the pack. And you know what? I don't want him to come back."

"Stop."

"No, for real. He's losing his mind, Odin. He said we need to hunt other Carnies."

Odin stirred, recalling his conversation with Dino Mike. "Was he serious?"

"Very. He said we need to go after them before they come after us. I don't know if I can be around someone who thinks that way."

Odin hesitated. "I don't know what to say."

"Do you think he's right? Are Carnies going to eat other Carnies?"

"No," Odin said. "I won't allow it."

"What are we going to do then?"

Odin sighed. "I've given that a lot of thought lately. Now, I haven't talked to Betty about this yet, so don't you dare tell her, but I think it might be time for us to leave the Good Lands."

"And go where?" Delilah said.

"I don't have it all worked out yet," said Odin. "But I don't see any other way. We can't sit around and starve to death. We need to be proactive."

Delilah's focus fell on Odin's hand. She put hers on top of his and looked Odin in the eye. "Let's go, then. I want to go with you."

"I hadn't planned on leaving you behind," Odin said. He tried to pull away, but Delilah held him down.

"Just you," Delilah said. "And me."

Odin's eyebrows shot up. "Delilah, I . . ."

Delilah's pupils dilated to the size of the moon. "I'll do whatever you say, Odin. We can start a new pack together and leave everything else behind."

"Odin!" Betty yelled. Odin jumped and nearly bumped his head on a star. He ran his hand through his feathers and cleared his throat several times.

"Relax," Delilah snarked. "It's not like she's here. You don't have to go."

"I do," Odin said. "I want to."

Delilah pouted. "But you didn't give me an answer."

"To what?" Odin said. "There's no question here."

"Odin!" Betty yelled again. "Where are you?"

"Odin!" Dino Mike shouted. "Odin! Come quick!"

Delilah and Odin exchanged worried looks.

Odin flew around a corner and almost knocked Dino Mike over. Dino Mike fixed his footing. Betty reeled Odin in. Tears streamed down her face.

"What's wrong?" Odin asked.

"Nothing," said Betty. She turned Odin's head by the jaw. Odin fell to his knees. The eggs rocked in the nest. A small crack crept up the side of one of them, like the onset of an earthquake. A spiderweb of cracks spread over the other. "They're hatching," Betty said.

Odin tackled Betty with a hug. His eyes were wetter than hers. They sat up together, eager to witness the miracle of life.

Delilah made her way to the clearing. "What's going on?" she asked.

"It's happening," Dino Mike said.

A small chunk dislodged from the first egg. Odin peeled it away. The world's tiniest orange snout snuck out and claimed its first ever breath of certified fresh air. Betty clamped and cut Odin's circulation off at the wrist.

Dino Mike's grin was permanent. He couldn't recall Betty ever weeping so much. Never had he ever seen Odin cry at all. Delilah attempted to smile, but a wave of sadness washed over her. Dino Mike pulled her in for a hug. To his surprise, she hugged him back. In reality, she was ready to out-cry them all. She just didn't want anyone to see. Odin flashed Delilah a quick, melancholy smile and pulled Betty in for a kiss. Delilah shoved Dino Mike.

"Excuse me," Delilah said. Dino Mike went to say something, but Delilah was gone.

The top half of the first egg was missing. A fuzzy orange head wobbled with mussy, blue feathers. Had the colors been inverted, the infant would've been a spitting image of Dino Mike.

A petite set of claws poked through the second egg's walls. Betty whimpered. The eggshell disintegrated. A doll-size version of Betty shook her head like a puppy.

"It's a female!" Betty said.

"This one too!" said Odin. "Two little girls."

Betty scooped the infants up and pressed them against her heart. Odin wrapped his arms around all three and hugged the stuffing out of them.

"Odin," Betty choked.

"Sorry," Odin said. He loosened his grip and kissed his daughters' heads.

"Congratulations," Dino Mike said. "Both of you. You're going to be great at this."

"Not just us," said Betty. "Congratulations to you too, Uncle Mike."

"Uncle Mike," Dino Mike said. He swelled with pride. "Sure has a nice ring to it."

## CHAPTER SIX
# DINO MIKE'S DYNAMITE PLAN

A sharp pain shot through the nerves in Dino Mike's ankle. He woke up and glanced down. Baby Fern, his pint-size carbon copy, pacified him with her innocent ocular organs.

"Aw, good morning, munchkin butt," Dino Mike said. He reached to stroke Fern's head. She clamped down on his finger with a dung-eating grin. "Ow." Dino Mike put his finger in his mouth. The wound failed to penetrate his skin. "Hungry, are you?"

"Morning, Uncle Mike," Betty said. She hoisted Fern from behind and slathered her with kisses. Fern wiped away as many as she could. Her sister, Ash, was clinging to Betty's hip.

"Morning," Dino Mike mumbled back. He thrust his arms and legs in opposite directions and held up a hand to gauge the sun. "Afternoon, rather. Did Odin leave without me?"

Betty pivoted. Odin was sprawled out in bed behind her.

"I gave him the day off," Betty said. "You should take one too. It's not every day we get to welcome two new members to the pack."

"Thanks, but Fern told me she was hungry," Dino Mike said. He showed Betty his finger. "I think I'll go fetch her and Ash some food."

"Oh yeah?" said Betty.

"Yeah," said Mike. "Maybe I'll have some luck without Odin slowing me down."

Betty tittered. Dino Mike was glad she did. He didn't want to tell her the real reason he wanted to go alone. Before he left, there was one last thing he had to clear up.

"Has anyone heard from Shank?" Dino Mike said.

"Not yet," said Betty. "But don't worry. He'll come around when he's ready."

It was hardly the answer Dino Mike was looking for. He would have felt better knowing Shank's whereabouts. At least then he wouldn't have had to risk running into him.

\* \* \*

Dino Mike tapped his elbow with the rolled-up map. The field of giant ferns beckoned him. It was a simple plan, really. He would shut his eyes, drag his feet, and grid search the plot in its entirety. Time wasn't an issue. It didn't matter if it took twenty minutes or the rest of the night. He was going to find that jagged rock.

In theory, Dino Mike's strategy was solid. In practice, it proved to be full of holes. For starters, with his eyes closed, or even with them open, he was quick to lose track of where he had searched and where he hadn't. He also hadn't accounted for there being multiple rocks hidden amongst the ferns. He investigated each one by scanning for prints and dusting for quills. A few hours and several dozen stone suspects later, Dino Mike was ready to give up.

Eventually, the ferns tapered off. Dino Mike's toes dangled over a precipice. An abrupt drop-off offered a breathtaking landscape he could look at but couldn't touch. Treetops ran like carpet, doubling as a canopy for the jungle below. A wide chasm carved through a pair of twin mountain peaks, bisecting them at their most symmetrical point. Dino Mike sucked on an incisor. He held his map up. The resemblance between the mountains and zigzags was uncanny.

Dino Mike's foot slipped over the edge of the cliff. He flapped his wings, kicked his planted heel, and fell back onto solid ground. Lying there, he clutched his heart with the balled-up map in his grasp and detected motion in his periphery. The Heterodontosaurus from the waterfall limped out of the ferns, stretched an arm over his head, and massaged an oblique.

"Hey!" Dino Mike shouted. The Heterodontosaurus's quills stood up. "Relax, it's me," Dino Mike said. "From the waterfall. Remember?"

The Heterodontosaurus held a clawed finger up to make a point. Before he made it, he squirted back into the ferns.

Dino Mike threw his arms up. "What did I say?"

In the ferns, the Heterodontosaurus peeked over his shoulder to make sure he hadn't been followed, and he paused to catch his wind. Three breaths later, he took a step forward and ran into something solid.

"Why are you running?" Dino Mike said.

The Heterodontosaurus hissed, trying to look mean.

"Really?" said Dino Mike.

The Heterodontosaurus slumped and ditched the façade. A hummingbird hovered near Dino Mike's head.

"Look! A bird!" the Heterodontosaurus said.

Dino Mike frowned. "No, seriously, it's right behind you."

Dino Mike gave in and turned. The hummingbird hovered to his other side. The Heterodontosaurus chuckled and pointed. Dino Mike turned again, but the hummingbird whirred back. Dino Mike glared at the Heterodontosaurus.

"Are you done?" Dino Mike asked.

The Heterodontosaurus wiped his face. With a last-ditch burst, he tried to run again, but Dino Mike snared him by the ankle and held him upside down.

"Why are you running?" Dino Mike said.

From where the Heterodontosaurus was hanging, Dino Mike might as well have been Shank Nightcuss. The Heterodontosaurus's eyes rolled back and his body went limp. Dino Mike shook his head and loosened his grip. The Heterodontosaurus landed with a thud.

The hummingbird returned and perched on a fern. It chirped a most pleasant tune. Dino Mike blinked and did a double take to make sure he wasn't seeing things. He laughed from deep in his belly, realizing the Herbie had been telling the truth.

\* \* \*

Blue and orange blurs circled the Heterodontosaurus in a feather-shucking zoetrope. The world stopped spinning, and Dino Mike and the dead bird came into focus.

"Agh!" the Heterodontosaurus yelled. He hopped up and ran, but his feet were ripped out from under him. Wincing, he reached for his ankle. A rope of braided vines bound him to a tree.

"I'm not going to hurt you. I just want to ask a few questions," Dino Mike said. He put the bird down and picked up the rope. "If I cut you free, do you promise not to run away?"

"Do you promise you're not going to eat me?" the Heterodontosaurus said.

"Um, no," Dino Mike said. "I mean, yes. I promise. Gross."

The Heterodontosaurus was offended. "What's that supposed to mean?"

"I don't eat other dinosaurs," Dino Mike said. "Like, ever. At all."

"Is that why you're so skinny?" the Heterodontosaurus asked.

"You know, maybe I'll just cut you free after," said Dino Mike. He let go of the rope.

"No, wait," the Heterodontosaurus said. He crossed his fingers behind his back. "Please. I won't run. I give you my word."

Dino Mike flicked out a claw. Sweat beaded on the Heterodontosaurus's throat. Dino Mike pulled the rope taut and sawed, one strand at a time. The rope snapped, and Mike folded his claw. He held his palms out and took a big step back.

The Heterodontosaurus kicked his foot free. He calculated the distance to the ferns and weighed the rate of his acceleration against the probability of his death.

Dino Mike held the map up. "I think this might belong to you," he said.

"Where did you get that?" the Heterodontosaurus said. He forgot all about the ferns.

"You dropped it at the waterfall," said Dino Mike.

The Heterodontosaurus tapped his fingers together. "Could I have it back?"

"Sure," Dino Mike said. He held the map out. The Heterodontosaurus reached for it, but Dino Mike pulled it back. "One or two conditions."

"What might those be?"

"I want to know what it leads to. And I want to know who or what a Poseidon is."

"No deal," the Heterodontosaurus said.

"Oh, come on," said Dino Mike. "You owe me. I saved your life the other day."

"By trying to eat me?"

"By scaring away the raptors. I told you, I don't eat other dinosaurs."

"What do you eat?" the Heterodontosaurus asked.

"Other things. Birds, fish, mammals. Eggs. I really love eggs. They're my favorite."

The Heterodontosaurus hesitated. "If I tell you where it goes, you'll give it back?"

"Of course," Dino Mike said.

The Heterodontosaurus sighed. "It's the way to the Great Lands."

"What's that?"

"An oasis in the Bad Lands. It's where we live now."

"Who's we?"

"Who do you think?"

Dino Mike was stunned. The Heterodontosaurus snatched the map. Dino Mike held out his empty hand. "I'm Michael Deinonychus. My friends call me Dino Mike."

The Heterodontosaurus responded without shaking. "Spinx. Groober Spinx."

"Good to know you, Mr. Spinx."

"If you say so, Mr. Deinonychus. Are we done here?"

"Almost. You didn't tell me who Poseidon is."

"And I'm not going to," said Groober. "You can't find the Great Lands without him. You'll get lost if you try."

"I don't see what the big deal is," Dino Mike said. "We've established trust. You know I don't eat dinosaurs."

"Yes, for reasons I don't quite understand, you've made that abundantly clear," said Groober. "But even if you don't, I'm certain your friends do."

"I don't really have any friends, to be honest."

"Then who is it that refers to you as Dino Mike?"

Dino Mike twirled the hummingbird's last remaining feather and plucked it away. "Are you hungry?"

Groober's face curled. "I happen to be a vegetarian."

"I wish I were," Dino Mike said. "That would make life easy."

"Maybe you are. I've never met a Carnie who didn't eat Herbies."

"That doesn't mean I eat plants," Dino Mike said. "Plants make Carnies sick."

"Is that a fact?"

"Of course it is. Everyone knows that."

Groober shucked a meaty branch from a low-hanging bush and bit off a leaf. He offered the branch to Dino Mike. "If you've never tried, how do you know?"

Dino Mike inspected the branch. It didn't look edible, but Groober's point was valid. "All right. I'll take a bite of the plant if you take a bite of the bird."

"You must not understand the term vegetarian. If I eat meat, I'll fall ill."

"Is that what happened last time?" Dino Mike asked.

"There was no . . ." Groober paused. Dino Mike wore a smug grin. "Touché," Groober said.

Dino Mike passed Groober a drumstick. Groober covered his mouth and fought to keep his bite of leaf from coming back up.

"No, seriously, I'm good," Groober said. "You don't have to eat the shrub."

"I want to try it now," Dino Mike said. "If I don't get sick, then my family doesn't have to starve."

"I don't see an incentive to participate," said Groober.

"You don't think it would benefit Herbies if Carnies could eat trees?"

Groober moaned and dangled the drumstick between two claws. "Okay, but this is for scientific purposes only."

Dino Mike nodded. He took a whiff of the branch and his stomach shriveled like a prune. "Just one bite."

"Are you sure you don't want to take two?" Groober asked.

"On three," said Mike. "One. Two. Three."

Dino Mike crunched down on the branch. Groober Spinx bit into the poultry. They chewed uncomfortably, their faces dripping with sweat.

"Mmm," Dino Mike said.

"Mm-hmm," mumbled Groober.

The chewing stopped. Awkward, forced swallows followed. Dino Mike stuck out his tongue. "Thee? That wuthn't tho bad."

"Exquisite," said Groober.

Their stomachs churned. The jig was up. Dino Mike and Groober turned away from each other and threw up in opposite bushes.

Dino Mike wiped his mouth. "I don't know how you guys do it."

"Please," Groober said. "Don't ever make me do that again." He burped and held a hand up to the sun. "It's getting late. I've got to rest. Got a long, dry road ahead of me. It's nice to have met you, Mr. Deinonychus. Thank you for returning my map. I would've had a hard time finding home without it."

"No problem," Dino Mike said. "Maybe I'll see you around."

"Don't count on it," said Groober. He started for the ferns.

"Hey, what happens if you get thirsty out there?" Dino Mike asked.

"I'll drink from a cactus," Groober said.

"A cactus?"

"Yeah, cactuses retain water. Isn't science cool?"

\* \* \*

Odin lay at the foot of his slab with his face in the dirt. Betty and the girls were curled in a ball on the bed above him.

"Odin," Dino Mike whispered. He tugged Odin's arm. It latched on to his wrist like a cobra. "Ouch. Odin. You're hurting me."

"Michael?" Odin said. He sat up groggily and let Dino Mike go. "What were you thinking sneaking up on me like that?"

"I'm sorry," Dino Mike said. "I didn't want to wake you. I just wanted to leave this for Ash and Fern." He held up the raw, one-legged hummingbird.

Odin rubbed his eyes. Betty's face twitched. She lifted her head and squinted.

"Is that real?" Betty said.

Dino Mike smiled. "I told you earlier. Fern said she was hungry."

Betty smiled. Odin grinned in disbelief. Dino Mike offered the bird to Betty, but she pushed it back.

"No," Betty said. "I'll wake the girls. You should give it to them."

Betty nudged her babies. Ash opened her eyes and yawned with delight. Fern wiggled her nose and rolled the other way. Dino Mike baited Fern with a sliver of meat. Her eyes sprang open and she pounced, reducing the slice to shreds.

"Sure got some spunk to her, doesn't she?" Dino Mike said.

Ash rappelled down Betty's feathers. Fern boxed her out, refusing to share.

"Aw," Dino Mike said. He placed a piece of bird on the slab at Ash's feet. Her face lit up with joy. Dino Mike broke down the bird and split up the rest of the meat.

Odin scooched over and rubbed Betty's shoulders. Betty rolled her neck back, enjoying every second of it. Dino Mike looked around. Delilah was still conked out in the same position he'd seen her in last. Shank remained missing in action.

Ash and Fern gnawed on bird bone. The meat had evaporated. Dino Mike's heart broke in two. He didn't know how long it would be until his nieces could eat again.

Dino Mike cleared his throat. "I know where the Herbies are," he said.

Odin stopped rubbing. Betty straightened her neck. "Come again?" Odin said.

"The Herbies," said Dino Mike. "They're hiding in the Bad Lands. The Great Lands, actually. But those are in the Bad Lands."

Odin slid past Betty and dropped two fists on Dino Mike's shoulders. "I'm sorry, Michael. I'm having a hard time hearing you."

"No, you're not," Dino Mike said. "You're having trouble comprehending. But it's the truth. Straight from the Herbie's mouth."

"What Herbie?" Odin asked.

"The one I found by the waterfall the day I lost the eggs. Funny-looking little guy. Head to toe, covered in quills."

"That explains those strange tracks," Betty said.

"You spoke with it?" said Odin.

"Well, not exactly," Dino Mike lied.

"Why didn't you kill it?"

"I tried," Dino Mike said. "He got away. He left a map behind, though, and I'm certain it leads to them."

"What map?" Betty asked. "Can we see it?"

"I sort of lost it," said Dino Mike. He ducked out from under Odin and flicked out a claw. "I can draw it, though. It's not that complicated."

Dino Mike dragged his claw and recreated Groober's map in the dirt. "These are the mountains here. I went today to investigate. It was a perfect match."

"What are the rest of those?" Betty asked.

"Landmarks, I'm sure," Dino Mike said. "I think the circle is where we have to go. The only thing I don't understand is this part at the top: *'Follow Poseidon.'* I'm not sure what that means, but I'm pretty sure it's the key to the whole shebang."

"Why didn't you tell us about this earlier?" Odin said.

"Because you were mad at me enough that day," said Dino Mike. "But that doesn't matter anymore. This is the solution to all of our problems."

"How do you figure?" said Odin. "We don't know if it's real or not. Who's to say this Herbie didn't drop the map on purpose so we'd get lost in the desert and die? They'd get a good laugh out of that, wouldn't they?"

"I don't understand," Dino Mike said. "Isn't this what you wanted? You said yourself it was time to consider leaving the Good Lands."

"What's he talking about?" Betty asked.

"Nothing," said Odin. "He's rehashing hypotheticals we can discuss later. That was before the girls were born, anyway. They wouldn't last a day in the desert."

Dino Mike bit his lip. "I didn't think of that," he said.

"There's a lot you don't think of," said Odin. "Do us all a favor: leave the thinking to me."

"I'll go," Dino Mike said. "If we can't all go, I'll go. I'll go into the desert. I'll find the Herbies. And when I find them, I'm going to bring them all back home with me."

"Great plan," Odin said sarcastically. "What are you going to tell them?"

"What if I just say we won't eat them anymore?" Dino Mike said. "There can't be a lot of food or water out there. They probably want to come back as it is."

"If he weren't your brother, I swear I'd eat him right now," Odin said. "I'm going back to bed. Tomorrow, we're finding that funny little Herbie and having him for funny little supper."

"Odin, please," Dino Mike said.

"I don't want to hear another word," said Odin. "You really messed up this time."

"Betty?" said Dino Mike.

Betty sighed. "He's right, Michael. It's a terrible idea, and you should have told us about the Herbie sooner."

"You don't mean that," Dino Mike said.

"I do," said Betty. "Go to bed. We'll discuss this in the morning."

* * *

Ash and Fern snuggled with Betty and Odin. Visions of hummingbirds flapped in their heads.

Dino Mike sloshed the snot from his nose and wiped a tear from his eye. He hoped Betty and Odin would forgive him for what he was about to do, but more so, he hoped Ash and Fern wouldn't forget about him if he didn't come back. At the very least, he hoped Betty would tell them stories about how brave their Uncle Mike was.

With a quivering breath, Dino Mike trekked into the woods. He took one determined step after another, until his foot rolled out from underneath him. Dino Mike groaned and rubbed his tush. It was a spear he had fallen over, probably the one Shank had brought too close to the nest.

Past the field of giant ferns, Dino Mike stood on the edge of the cliff, holding the spear like a staff. The sky was starry and lucid. The moon was super, full, bright. It hung between the twin mountain peaks.

Dino Mike knelt on the bank of a modest pond and sipped from the water's surface. The desert beyond the mountains had come into focus, and it was already making him thirsty.

The ground shook. Dino Mike tilted his head. A Sauroposeidon some sixty feet tall ambled by on all fours. The silhouette of its cumbersome neck passed over the moon. With a mouthful of molars, the Sauroposeidon chomped the head off a tree. Dino Mike gasped.

"Who's down there?" the Sauroposeidon bellowed. Vegetation spewed from his mouth.

Dino Mike dropped his spear and put his hands up. "I . . . uh, just me. I was just passing by. I mean you no harm."

The Sauroposeidon boomed with laughter. Flocks of birds fled for their lives.

"What's so funny?" Dino Mike asked.

"No offense, dude," the Sauroposeidon said, "but what harm could you possibly cause me?"

"Right," said Dino Mike. "What I meant to say was please don't hurt me."

"Why would I do that?" said the Sauroposeidon. "I'm a pretty docile creature."

"I'm sorry," said Dino Mike. "You're just so big."

"That's what happens when you eat your veggies."

Dino Mike scratched his neck. "Look, my name's Dino Mike, but my friends call me, uh, Dino Mike. Anyway, I'd shake your hand but—"

The Sauroposeidon lifted one of the tree trunks he called legs and offered up a hoof. "Name's Poseidon. Nice to meet you, dude. Go on, give me some. Bump the rock."

Dino Mike pounded the rock, or boulder rather, considering it was larger than him. "Wait a sec," Dino Mike said. "Poseidon? You're Poseidon?"

"Yep."

"The Poseidon?"

"Nope."

"What do you mean nope?"

"Not the Poseidon. Just Poseidon. I would never put an article in front of my name. Can you imagine the arrogance?"

"I can't tell if you're being modest or if that means there are two of you," Dino Mike said.

"There are more than two Poseidons," said Poseidon. "Every Sauroposeidon is named Poseidon, but I assure you, there's only one of me."

"You all have the same name?"

"Yep."

"Why? That sounds confusing."

"Who knows? Maybe our ancestors couldn't process more than one name with their tiny, little brains,"

Poseidon said. "On the plus side, it makes things easy to remember."

"Where are the others?" Dino Mike asked.

"Migrated. It's mating season."

"Why aren't you with them?"

"Because I'm not ready to mate. I went last year, and I didn't have anything to do. It's not worth taking a trip that could kill me."

"How bad could it be?"

"You ever been to the Bad Lands?" Poseidon said. "Our mating grounds are a week away at least, and there isn't any food or water along the way. A lot of us die trying to get there. Seems like a waste when there are perfectly good trees right here." Poseidon bit off another treetop.

"Do you know anything about a place called the Great Lands?" Dino Mike asked. "Some other Herbies supposedly live there. It's supposed to be in the Bad Lands."

"Not in this desert, dude. I promise you. There's nothing but death."

"But I saw a map that leads to it."

"Never heard a word about it," Poseidon said.

"That's funny, because it had your name right on top," said Dino Mike. "And this symbol." He picked up the spear and drew seven circles on the ground. "It said *'Follow Poseidon'* right next to it."

"Those aren't symbols," Poseidon said. "They're stars."

"Stars? Those stars?" Dino Mike asked. He pointed to the cluster he'd matched up before.

"Yep. That's Poseidon too. We follow him because he always knows which way to go."

"I don't get it," Dino Mike said.

"Do I have to connect the dots for you?" said Poseidon.

Dino Mike squinted, and everything made sense. He connected the circles by drawing a line with his spear. They formed a big-bodied dinosaur with a long neck and tail. It looked just like Poseidon.

"It's a constellation," Dino Mike said.

"Get this dinosaur a prize," said Poseidon.

"That's it, then," said Dino Mike. "I have to follow the constellation."

"I don't know about that," Poseidon said.

"Thank you so much," Dino Mike continued. "Seriously. I can't thank you enough."

"Where are you going?" Poseidon asked.

"To the Great Lands. I have a family to feed."

"Okay. Good luck. Try not to die out there."

"I don't intend to," Dino Mike said. "Thanks again, friend."

Dino Mike took one last breath and let it out with a whoosh. He looked up, stepped out, and followed the Poseidon constellation through the mountains into the Bad Lands.

"Yep, he's going to die," Poseidon said. He took a fresh bite of tree and chewed with his mouth open. "What a brave, dumb, little dude."

CHAPTER SEVEN
## THE BAD LANDS

A rickety tumbleweed hitched a ride on the tail of a blustery nighttime breeze. Dino Mike shivered. It was the closest thing to a sign of life he'd seen since he left the Good Lands, other than the occasional cactus or patch of Joshua trees. The loneliness didn't get to him though. He was used to isolation. It was the near-freezing temperature he had trouble dealing with. No one ever mentioned how cold the Bad Lands got after dark, not that Dino Mike could recall anyway. He had enough to worry about as it was. A chapped, runny nose wasn't what he signed up for.

Behind Dino Mike, a trail of footprints traipsed to infinity. Overhead, his only friend, Poseidon, was fading from the sky. Sunrays curled on the horizon, taunting Dino Mike with the prospect of thawed blood vessels. He let the warmth wash over his face. It felt good, but he knew it wouldn't last. Before long, the blistering heat of the day would reduce his body to jerky. He needed to seek shelter. A trio of mushroom-shaped rock formations seemed to offer just that.

Dino Mike set his spear down and sat against one of the hoodoo's walls. Fourteen angry eyelids snapped open, and fourteen beady pupils flitted like synchronized swimmers. A humongous, ticked-off scorpion scuttled over. It snapped a pair of pincer-clad pedipalps and pumped its venom-tipped tail. Dino Mike bit his lip. The scorpion's claws sure looked meaty.

Under the shade of his new jumbo-size umbrella, Dino Mike kicked back and picked his teeth with the scorpion's tail. With a hard-earned yawn, he flicked the stinger to the side, crossed his legs, and folded his arms under his neck. Satisfied, he allowed his eyelids to close, and a genuine smile fell over his face.

*　*　*

A gruff gust of wind ruffled Dino Mike's feathers, plucking him from what must have been a most pleasant dream. Dino Mike went to yawn and choked on dirt instead. It was midday, but the desert was dim. Sheets of dust pulled like curtains through the air.

Two miniature tornadoes chased each other in circles. Dino Mike grinned. The funnels reminded him of Ash and Fern. They evaporated though, and his smile went with them. It wrenched his gut missing those little boogers.

Something bumbled along like any other tumbleweed. As it passed by, however, Dino Mike realized it wasn't a weed at all. It was a leaf, one that was folded and creased.

"No way," Dino Mike said. He hopped up. The ground scalded the pads of his feet. "Yee-ouch!" Dino Mike clung to the side of his stone mushroom. The leaf spun in an invisible cyclone. Dino Mike grabbed his spear and drew a breath. He didn't have a choice. He couldn't let the leaf get away.

"Ah! Ooo! Eee! Agh!" Dino Mike hotfooted like the ground was made of burning coal. Using his spear, he pinned the fledgling down. The edges curled, and the words *Follow Poseidon* confirmed his suspicion.

Dino Mike reached for the map. It brushed against his fingertips before the wind whipped up and whisked it away. Dino Mike frowned, but he didn't have time to dwell on it. He looked up, and something resembling static multiplied like bacteria in the distance. Mike scratched his head. It was murky, whatever it was. It was also coming his way.

"Oh, dung."

Dino Mike dashed. A tsunami of dirt swarmed like locusts, devouring everything in its wake. Whole feathers were ripped from Dino Mike's body. Debris stung him in the face like a horde of angry bees. Dino Mike churned his legs and forced his heart to pump double. He was afraid if he slowed down, the storm would wash him away completely.

The tidal wave broadened, blacking out the sun. Dino Mike squinted. He swore he saw a crevice in a foothill a quarter mile ahead. He laid odds in favor of it being a cave but bet against being able to make it there in time. Nevertheless, he altered his course and turned up the jets. The freight train roared behind him, uprooting cactuses and overturning boulders at his heels. With his visibility approaching zero, Dino Mike confirmed the cave's existence but realized he'd grossly overestimated its size. Running at full speed, Dino Mike covered his head and dove. His body squeaked through the almost nonexistent aperture and skidded over an abrasive stone floor. The dust storm pulverized the desert outside.

Dino Mike pressed his back against a cold wall and examined his head like a certified phrenologist. He couldn't see anything, but his skull was intact. In fact, he'd survived with only scratches, a few lost feathers, and a pair of skinned-up knees. When his senses adjusted, he noticed a shuddering lump next to him. He reached out to touch it, and something pricked his finger.

"Ow!" Dino Mike said. He stuck his finger in his mouth, and the flavor of rust flooded his taste buds. "Groober?"

"Who's there?" Groober Spinx said. "I'm warning you, I'm armed, and I'm dangerous."

"I knew it. It's me, Dino Mike."

"Who?" The roaring storm made it difficult to hear.

"Dino Mike!"

"The deinonychus? What are you doing here?"

"What?"

"Why are you here?"

"It's storming outside!"

"What?" Groober said.

"It's storming outside!"

"Hadn't noticed!" said Groober. "What are you doing in the Bad Lands?"

"The what?"

"The Bad Lands! Why are you here?"

Dino Mike stalled. He understood the question. He just couldn't tell Groober the truth without blowing up his plan. "I can't hear you!"

"What?" Groober said.

Dino Mike cupped his hands. "I can't hear you! Let's talk later!"

Groober covered his ear and shoved Dino Mike.

\* \* \*

Moonlight slithered through the crack at the entrance of the cave. Dino Mike's eyelids opened. Groober was drooling on his shoulder. Other than Groober's snoring, though, Dino Mike didn't hear a thing. Gently, he lifted Groober's head and laid it on the ground.

Dino Mike limped out of the cave. The air was still and nippy. A thousand million stars glinted about the celestial highways overhead. Dino Mike rubbed his shoulders. There were a few overturned cactuses in the vicinity, but, other than that, there was little to suggest there had been a storm at all.

Dino Mike licked the roof of his mouth. It tasted like sandpaper. He eyeballed a brittle chunk of cactus at his feet. *I'll drink from a cactus,* he recalled Groober saying. *Cactuses retain water. Isn't science cool?* Dino Mike gripped his spear.

Groober Spinx waddled out of the cave wearing a mammal-skin poncho. Dino Mike held the skewered cactus chunk up and let a droplet of milk dribble onto his tongue. It was putrid and bitter, and he spit it out immediately. Groober busted his gut.

"What's so funny?" Dino Mike asked. "And what are you wearing?"

"This old thing?" said Groober. "One-hundred-percent mammal. Say what you want about them being an inferior species. They know how to stay warm at night."

"At what cost?" said Dino Mike. "You look ridiculous."

"That means a lot coming from you," said Groober. "You do know cactus water is non-potable, right?"

"Non-pota what?"

"Not drinkable. Unless you want to vomit or get diarrhea. It makes you sick."

Dino Mike scrubbed his tongue with his shoulder. "Why did you say you could drink it?"

"I did no such thing."

"Yes, you did. In the Good Lands, when I asked what you'd do if you got thirsty."

"Clearly that was a joke," Groober said. "It is a common misconception, am I right?"

Mike slung the cactus at Groober, who bent at the knees and dodged like a magus. He straightened his back and adjusted his sleeves. Dino Mike wasn't impressed.

"If I can't drink that, what can I drink?" Dino Mike said. "I'm shriveling up."

"There is water in the desert. You just have to know where to look," said Groober. He meandered about, browsing the arid terrain. "There," he said, pointing matter-of-factly.

"There, what?" said Dino Mike. All he saw was a tiny, dried-up twig. "Is this another one of your jokes?"

Groober dug around the base of the twig. It was longer than it first appeared. He coiled it twice and gave it a tug. A bulbous root squirted out of the ground like a turnip.

"Whoa," Dino Mike said. "Is that full of water?"

"Sort of," said Groober. He pulled a flat rock from under his poncho and filed the side of the root. Shavings accrued like sawdust at his feet. Dino Mike was repulsed. "What's the matter?" Groober asked. "I thought you were thirsty?"

"I am. But I want to drink water, not wood."

"Suit yourself. More for me." Groober packed a handful of shavings into a ball, held it over his mouth, and clenched his fist. Nothing happened.

"Great," Dino Mike said. "You've lost it."

Groober shook his hand and squeezed some more. Fluid trickled into his mouth. He gargled and swallowed.

"Ahh. That's refreshing," Groober said.

Dino Mike didn't waste any time. He strangled a handful of shavings over his mouth and inhaled a mixture of sawdust and water. Seven or eight root balls later, he unleashed a burp.

"You know what, Groober?" Dino Mike said. "You're all right. I don't care what I say about you."

Groober belched. "Your approval means the world."

Poseidon twinkled in the sky.

"I'd better get moving," said Groober. "You'd better get home."

"I think we might be headed the same way, actually," Dino Mike said. "Why don't we just roll together?"

"The Good Lands are that way," said Groober. "That's not where I'm going."

"Me neither," said Dino Mike. He pointed up. "I'm going where he's going."

"You can't be serious," said Groober.

"As a toothache," said Dino Mike.

"No, no, no. You can't. You don't even eat dinosaurs, so why would you want to?"

"Maybe I just need a change of scenery."

"Your needs are irrelevant. If anyone were to see you, they would put an end to you, do you understand? Then they would put me on trial to determine if I was complicit."

"Who's they?" Dino Mike asked.

"Don't play dumb with me, Mr. Deinonychus. Herbies aren't big fans of Carnies. Never have been."

Dino Mike smiled. "Very well, Mr. Spinx. But I wasn't asking to join you. I was inviting you to join me. Unless you think you can make it there without a map."

"I have a map," Groober said. He fumbled around under his poncho but came up empty-handed.

"Right," said Dino Mike. He turned his nose up and marched. "Don't worry. I won't let them know it was you who showed me the way."

Furious, Groober kicked the first thing he could. Unfortunately, it was a cactus.

"Agh!"

\* \* \*

Dino Mike flicked an icicle from his nostril. The night was frigid, and the desert grew colder the farther he and Groober went. Their lack of conversation only added to the clamminess. Dino Mike glared at Groober's poncho with disdain but didn't say a word. Groober was smug enough as it was. He didn't need any more ammunition.

Groober halted. Dino Mike stopped too. Something crunched under his foot. He lifted his leg. Fragments of jawbone fell from his toes.

"Gross," Dino Mike said. "Is that what I think it is?"

"That's nothing," said Groober. He gestured into the darkness. A skeleton graveyard manifested before them. "We're here."

"Where is here exactly?"

"The haunted boneyard."

"What's it haunted by?"

"It isn't. We just say that so no one will visit. Let's make camp."

"We're staying here?" Dino Mike asked.

"We must," Groober said. "There's no more shelter from here to the water tree."

Dino Mike high-stepped over a spinal column and almost impaled himself on a rib. Bones were scattered everywhere. Most had been picked clean.

"Where did these all come from?" Dino Mike asked.

"This is as far as most dinosaurs make it in the Bad Lands," Groober said. "The ones who can't go any farther make their final stop here. Beats dying alone, I guess."

A draft reduced a tailbone to dust. "They're disintegrating," Dino Mike said.

"There's not much left to most of them. The sun does a number on the corpses. The scavengers take care of the rest."

"Scavengers?"

"Vultures mostly," said Groober. "Perhaps the occasional giant, ravenous beast." He waved an arm to present a garage-sized rib cage. Its walls were thatched with palm leaves and tar. "After you."

"You're too kind," said Dino Mike. He hunched his shoulders, entered, and blew in his hands for warmth. Groober held out one of his.

"What?" Dino Mike said. "You want me to blow on your hands too?"

"The map," said Groober. "I'll need it to plot tomorrow's course."

"I don't have it," Dino Mike said.

"Quit playing," said Groober. "You told me you had it back at the cave."

"No, I didn't. I said that you didn't. I knew because I watched it blow away."

Groober pulled Dino Mike down by the neck feathers. "I need that map, you idiot. I can't get home without it."

"Relax," Dino Mike said. He broke Groober's grip without trying. "I can draw the map. I do have to say, though, I'm shocked you don't have it memorized."

"I engineered a self-sustainable colony in the middle of an uninhabitable desert," Groober said. "You don't think I can remember three puny symbols?"

"What's the problem, then?"

"It wasn't just a map, drawn precisely to scale, I might add. It was a compass too."

"And?"

"And I . . ." Groober mumbled. He stared at the dirt. "I suffer from left/right confusion. I can't tell which is which."

"Wow. Sort of conflicts with your whole genius-slash-engineer pitch, does it not?"

"Intelligence has nothing to do with it," said Groober. "It's like directional dyslexia."

"What's it matter, anyway?" Dino Mike said. "Don't we just follow Poseidon?"

Groober dragged Dino Mike out of the rib cage and pointed to the sky. "Look. Poseidon's direction doesn't change. His body rotates around the sky, but his head always points north. If we follow him from here, we'd reach another jungle, eventually and in theory. But it's too far. Only sauropods can store enough calories to make a trek like that. We would die on the way."

"So we don't follow him?"

"We use him as a guide."

Dino Mike stroked his chin. With his spear, he scribbled a map in the dirt. "This is the water tree you spoke about?"

"It is," said Groober.

"Okay, well, it's to the right of us on the map. So, you're saying when we look up, we want to see Poseidon's head pointing right, right?"

Groober frowned. He looked down at the map and up at the sky. The Poseidon heads pointed in opposite directions. "The boneyard is east. Not right. Not left. The compass and the constellation have to point the same way."

Dino Mike wiped the map clean and started from scratch. This time, he aligned the dots with the stars. "Ah," Dino Mike said. "He's pointing north, which would be on our left if we were traveling east, which is to the right on the map. What's this to the west?"

"The tar pits," Groober said. "I don't know what you know about those, but tar pits and dinosaurs don't mix."

The wind blasted, chilling Dino Mike's spine. He shivered and swallowed his pride. "I don't suppose you have another one of those ponchos?"

"One of these silly things? Afraid not, sorry."

"Is there anything else I can do to keep from freezing to death?"

"You can start a fire," Groober said.

"I can," said Dino Mike.

"Sure," said Groober. "That bucket of tar's technically combustible. Go on. Blast it with a lightning bolt. That might do the trick."

"No. I mean, I can. Start a fire," Dino Mike said.

"No, you can't," said Groober. "Fires only occur in nature. I was being facetious."

"No, really. I can. I just have to rub two sticks together."

"That's absurd. And you only have one stick anyway."

Dino Mike snapped the spear over his knee. Groober was dumbfounded. "Isn't common sense cool?" Dino Mike said.

Groober crossed his arms. Dino Mike scooped some twigs and needles into a pile. He jammed one stick on top of the pile and strummed it with the other. Nothing happened. Groober gave a round of applause.

"Magnificent," Groober said. "Truly. Absolutely magnificent."

Dino Mike bit his tongue and fiddled harder. The sticks smoked. A spark shot off and sent the rubbish up in flames.

"Groober?" Dino Mike said.

Groober didn't respond. He couldn't believe his eyes.

"Groober!"

"Huh?"

"You're on fire!"

Smoke billowed under Groober's poncho. "Agh!" he screamed, and he ran like a raptor with its head cut off.

"Take it off!" Dino Mike said.

Groober pulled the poncho up, but it got stuck over his head. A slow-burning flame kissed his neck. "Agh!" he yelled again. He fell over and rolled until the fire went out. Dino Mike helped peel the smoking poncho away. The smell of singed hair hung in the air.

* * *

Abstract shadows danced around a campfire in a flame-retardant stone pit. Dino Mike and Groober huddled together, basking in the fire's warmth. Groober's poncho lay in a charred heap.

"Sorry about your coat, buddy," Dino Mike said.

"No worries," said Groober. "It was last year's model anyway." Something clattered like a rattlesnake's tail. Groober bounced. "Did you hear that?"

"I didn't hear anything," Dino Mike said. The rattle shook again. Groober hopped into Dino Mike's lap. "Ouch," Dino Mike said with a shove. "Groober, you're covered in quills."

"My bad," said Groober. "I forget sometimes. That sounded close, didn't it?"

"It was probably just the wind."

A terrifying new sound made Dino Mike hop on top of Groober. It was loud and distinct, like something sharp slicing through bone.

"That doesn't sound like wind to me," Groober said.

Dino Mike ripped a strip of fur from Groober's poncho and wrapped it around one end of a femur bone. He dipped the bone in the bucket of tar and dunked it in fire. It lit like a torch. Something dragged along a rib cage behind them and played a full scale of notes. Dino Mike spun and cast his flickering light.

"There's nothing there," Dino Mike said. He turned back, and his teeth chattered. "Groober, on your left!"

Groober looked to his right. Darkness.

"Your other left!"

Groober checked his shoulder. A hideous hand coiled around a rib cage. It had a fistful of blades where its fingers should have been. Each was over a meter long.

"Run!" Dino Mike said. Groober took off. Dino Mike checked Poseidon's heading and waved his torch. "Not that way, Groober!" he yelled. "Over here!" The scissor-handed monster snipped the air. Dino Mike split.

By the time Groober caught up with Mike, the campfire was but a speck in the distance. The two of them hunched over to catch their breath.

"What was that?" Dino Mike said.

"I haven't the faintest," said Groober. "I guess that place really is haunted."

"What do we do now?"

"We move on."

"I thought you said there wasn't any shelter?"

"There isn't," said Groober. "But we really don't have a choice now, do we?" He took the torch from Mike.

\* \* \*

In the distance, Groober's torch bounced along like a beacon in the night. In the foreground, a titanic, snarling head rose from the shadows.

Groober stopped in a thick patch of Joshua trees. "What is it?" Dino Mike said. "You want to make camp here?"

"No," said Groober. "I thought I heard something."

"Relax," said Dino Mike. "You're probably still jittery."

Groober waved the torch behind them. The flame bounced off an evil set of eyes.

"Oh, dung," Groober said.

An allosaurus charged, gnashing a gnarly set of teeth. Its mouth was big enough to swallow Groober whole. Groober fainted, leaving Dino Mike to fend for himself. The torch fell and rolled to the foot of a Joshua tree.

Dino Mike wanted to run, but he couldn't. Even if his conscience would've allowed him to leave Groober behind, the allosaurus was already too close. Mike scooped up the torch. A flaming wad of fur fell from the top.

The allosaurus closed in. The Joshua tree caught fire and ignited the others. Dino Mike roared and waved the torch in the predator's face. The allosaurus snapped its jaws. The bone splintered into thousands of pieces.

Dino Mike slumped. Groober Spinx slept. The tiny-armed allosaurus sneered. The blaze of Joshua trees walled off the exits. Dino Mike unhinged his claws and prepared to meet his maker. He looked the allosaurus in the eye. To his astonishment, the allosaurus blinked. Dino Mike was befuddled, until he realized the allosaurus wasn't looking at him but behind him. Dino Mike started to turn. A blunt object struck him in the back of his head, and the world went black.

CHAPTER EIGHT
# O MARKS THE SPOT

Thinning trails of smoke curled up from the remains of the smoldering Joshua trees. Brute Grimstone, a potbellied ankylosaurus, dragged his rugged club of a tail through the rubble, knelt, and rolled a lifeless mound of quills over.

"It's him," Brute said.

Taddle Bill, a sniveling Tenontosaurus with a stick and stone shovel, and Anna Van Kirk, a brawny Animantarx with gorgeous eyes and a face full of spikes, appeared at Brute's side.

"Is he alive?" Anna asked.

"I don't know," said Brute. He shook Groober by the shoulders. "Come on. Wake up, little buddy."

Groober's eyelids opened. He hacked out a chestful of dirt. "Brute?" Groober said.

"Phew," said Anna. She dropped a paw on Taddle Bill's shoulder. Taddle slid out from under it.

"It's me, pal," Brute said. "What happened? We saw the smoke all the way from the tree."

"Smoke?" said Groober. He scanned his memory bank. "Oh no."

"What the dung?" Taddle Bill blurted. With the head of his shovel, he prodded a mass of orange dust and blue feathers. Dino Mike's body was swollen, bloody, and blistered.

"Mr. Deinonychus!" Groober said. He hopped over Brute's tail and put an ear to Dino Mike's chest. It registered the faintest of beats. "He's alive."

Brute nodded. "Kill it," he said.

Taddle swung the shovel back. "No, wait!" Groober shouted. He flailed his arms. Taddle hooked his downstroke and carved a moon-shaped divot in the ground.

"Dadgummit, Spinx," Taddle said. "Are you trying to get yourself bludgeoned?"

"You can't kill him," said Groober.

"Why not?" said Anna.

"He's my . . . friend," said Groober. "He saved my life."

"The Carnie?" Brute asked. "From what?"

"An allosaurus," Groober said. Anna's eyebrows shot up. "I know. It sounds far-fetched," Groober continued. "I'm having trouble picturing it myself."

"You didn't see it?" said Brute.

"Not exactly," said Groober. "I lost consciousness. He must have used the fire to scare it away. The point is, we wouldn't be having this conversation if he hadn't."

"What are we even talking about here?" Taddle said. "He's a Carnie. Allosauri are Carnies. They were probably working in cahoots." Taddle wielded his shovel like a sword. "There could be more of them out there watching us right now."

"You see that knot on his head?" Groober said. "You don't get a lump like that from being in cahoots. He needs medical attention. We need to get him help."

"So he can make a snack of us when he's feeling better?" Taddle said. "No thank you."

"He won't eat us," said Groober. "He doesn't eat other dinosaurs."

"What makes you say that?" Anna said.

"He told me so," said Groober

"And you believe him?" said Anna.

"We spent a night in a cave together," Groober said. "He didn't eat me."

"I wouldn't exactly call you appetizing," said Brute.

"Not even for a starving Carnie in the middle of a desert?" said Groober.

"Maybe he didn't want to crap out your quills," said Taddle.

"What was he doing in the Bad Lands in the first place?" Anna asked.

"I don't know," Groober said. "I'd love to ask. But I can't if we don't help him."

"To be clear, you're saying we should take him back to the Great Lands?" Brute asked.

"So Harvey can ream us for not killing it?" Taddle argued. "No way. We have a schedule to keep."

"He's right," said Anna. "That's what Harvey would do and say."

"You don't think Harvey will want to know how he started the fire?" Groober said.

"He started it?" said Anna.

"Yeah," said Groober. "Didn't I mention that?"

\* \* \*

The song of an angel soared down from the heavens above. A blue-and-green-striped tail bounced to the beat of the cherubic tune, blending in with the twisted olive tree branches with which it was intertwined. Harmonica Anthophilous, a Parasaurolophus, dangled her legs over a bough. Her scales shimmered as she poured her soul through the dimpled crest on top of her head. As she sang, Harmonica shucked drupes from the tree and dropped them onto a net laid out like a blanket below.

Several others like it, already full, were rolled up against an adjacent tree.

A perfect olive hit the ground and took a funny bounce. It rolled away at a high rate of speed and nestled in a fort under a mass of tangled roots. Inside the fort, a group of rocks encircled a bed of leaves that housed a single oblong egg. A silky shadow slithered past. Sonny Pacquiao, a pint-size Pachycephalosaurus with a thick, bony crown, adjusted his shoulders and wiped his mouth. He held an ovoid rock in one hand and wiggled the fingers on his other. With one swift motion, he swapped the rock for the egg and marveled at his new treasure. An olive pelted Sonny in the back of the neck.

"Put Eggbert down, or you're going to scramble him," Harmonica said.

"But I got no one else to play with," Sonny whined.

"You can play with me," said Harmonica. "I'm playing get-the-olives-to-Contessa so she has time to get them ready for supper."

"I hate olives," said Sonny. He fell on the bed of leaves with Eggbert in his lap. "That's all we ever eat."

"Boohoo," said Harmonica. "At least the olives don't try to eat you." Harmonica looked up. A burly stegosaurus trampled over with a full head of steam and her nose held high.

"Harmonica," the stegosaurus snorted.

Harmonica rolled her eyes. "What can I do for you, Penny?"

"My brother needs to talk to you," Penny said.

"About what?"

"That's between you and him."

"I will see Harvey at suppertime," said Harmonica. "From a distance, across the table. If he absolutely must, he can try to speak to me then."

Penny flexed her muscles. Her biceps were huge. "He said it's urgent."

"Not as urgent as what I'm doing," Harmonica said. "Unless you want to drop the harvest off to Contessa and watch Sonny."

Penny shook Harmonica's tree, knocking enough olives loose to cover the rest of the net. She rolled the net up like a carpet and threw it over her shoulder. "Contessa can watch Sonny," Penny said. "I'll drop him off with the first load and come back for the rest."

Sonny pouted. Harmonica pursed her lips.

\* \* \*

On the surface of a small pond in the aorta of the Great Lands, water evaporated at a steady rate. The pond was the centerpiece of a mostly dry basin, with mineral-laced walls that warbled like bards spinning tales of better times and higher water levels. The olive grove spiraled around the top of one side.

"What took so long?" a stegosaurus said in a nasally voice. He was super-jacked and had a thick armor crust, but his head was too small for his body.

"Cut the crud, Harvey," Harmonica said. "What do you want?"

"A moss-and-conifer salad would be nice," said Harvey. "And with an attitude like that, you can call me Mr. Plates."

Miranda McBeek, a slender Abrictosaurus, rolled her eyes. She looked a lot like Groober, minus the quills, and barely came up to Harvey's stomach.

"I don't have time for this," Harmonica said.

"Actually, Harmonica, it was me who asked you here," said Miranda.

Harmonica smiled. "In that case, what can I do for you, Ms. McBeek?" Harvey frowned.

"I'm not going to spinach-coat this," Miranda said. "Things are getting bad." She held up a packet of crispy, brown leaves. The edges flaked off in the wind. "If there are any further delays, any at all, we're going to run out of water."

Harvey squeezed his head. "I told you there won't be any more delays."

"Now where have I heard that before?" said Miranda.

"The pump is built," Harvey said. "The trench is dug. The riverbed is all dammed up. All we need to do is lay the track to get the water from the tree to the bed and finish drilling. That's it. We're golden. It will flow here all by itself."

"Sounds groovy," Miranda said. "But you forgot to account for unforeseen circumstances."

"There. Won't. Be. Any," said Harvey. He spelled his words out in a faux sign language.

"How do you know?" Miranda said in actual sign language. "Can you foresee them?"

Harmonica checked the reservoir. The bottom of the pond was as clear as the top. Some rocks on the floor even broke the pond's surface. "Exactly how much water do we have?"

"Two and a half, maybe three weeks' worth if we don't replenish," Miranda said.

"That's it?" said Harmonica.

"That pond will be overflowing in two and a half, maybe three days," said Harvey.

Miranda and Harmonica pretended like Harvey wasn't there. "We can stretch it a bit further if we put a few conservation measures in place," Miranda said.

"What are we talking?" Harmonica asked.

"We could tighten up rations for starters," Miranda said. "Which is to say we'll need to implement rationing. And we must ban all uses of water other than drinking, immediately and indefinitely. No bathing. No swimming. No water fights, watering plants, or planting new seeds. I also think we should ask Contessa to cut back on the salt. It's making us thirstier."

"I can't grow food if I can't water," Harmonica said.

"And have Contessa use less salt?" said Harvey. "Her food is inedible as is."

"Unfortunately, you can't water plants if you've already died of thirst," Miranda said.

Harmonica broke down and looked to Harvey for an opinion. "Don't look at me," said Harvey. "I already told her she's crazy."

"No," Harmonica said. "She's pragmatic. And right."

"You'll see at the meteor shower," said Harvey. "We'll toast falling ember with natural springwater. Which reminds me, you still haven't gotten back to me about being my date."

"Was there a deadline?" Harmonica said. "What are the chances one of those embers falls on your head?"

"Consider your hat out of the ring," said Harvey.

"But I was so close," said Harmonica. "Seriously, are you going to talk to Granny about the water measures or not?"

"This place stinks bad enough," said Harvey. "You want to eighty-six baths?"

"Grow up. It's temporary," said Harmonica. "It's either that or I go talk to her about the other option, which is what everyone really wants to do."

"You wouldn't," said Harvey.

"I would, and I still might," said Harmonica. "Just do it, Harvey. There's got to be some reason why you're a leader. Do what's right for the herd. Don't put us at risk."

*　*　*

Groober Spinx scurried along the bank of a dry riverbed and gnawed on his hand. Dino Mike's body dangled over Brute's broad shoulders. The lump on his noggin was swollen and seeping with pus. Ahead, the riverbed wound into a whorl of densely packed palm trees and desert bamboo. Behind, Taddle and Anna brought up the rear. Taddle held his shovel close to his chest, ready and willing to knock Dino Mike's block off if he happened to wake up.

Anna peeked around a gargantuan palm. A well-worn path paved the way to a cul-de-sac of makeshift teepees varying greatly in size. There wasn't a Herbie in sight.

Brute and Groober hopscotched to the teepee at the top of the street. Groober pulled back the palm-leaf curtain, and Brute stuffed Dino Mike in. His body took up the whole tent. Groober wiggled in to examine Dino Mike's head.

"It's getting worse," Groober said. "We have to find Harmonica."

"Have fun with that," said Taddle. "I'm telling Harvey." With that, he was gone.

Groober pled with Anna and Brute. "Please," he said. "We have to find Harmonica before they get back."

"You'd better get going, then," said Anna.

"But he—wait, what?" said Groober.

"Seriously," said Brute. "Hurry up. Taddle won't be gone long."

"What if the Carnie wakes up?" Groober asked.

"I think we'll be all right," Brute said. A vein bulged in his neck.

\* \* \*

Groober stepped on an olive. It oozed through his toes like jam. He peered down several rows of olive trees like hallways but saw no sign of Harmonica.

"Great," Groober said.

A metric ton of olives sizzled over a commercial-size grill. The appliance itself wasn't heated; rather, the olives had been spread thinly over a bed of granite where they baked in the sun. Contessa Treehorn, a plump triceratops with saintly horns and a warm, loving smile, dusted the fruit with salt and a secret blend of signature herbs and spices.

"Yah!" Sonny Pacquiao screamed. He toted Eggbert like a football and hurdled the grill.

"Boy, listen here!" Contessa yelled, but Sonny squirted off. Contessa sighed heavily and popped an olive into her mouth. "Mmm."

"Contessa." Groober jostled over.

"Groober," said Contessa. "You're back."

"Just arrived," he said. "Have you seen Harmonica? It's urgent I speak with her."

Contessa's smile inverted. "She's at the reservoir, speaking to Harvey about some other urgent matter."

"Do you know what it was about?" Groober asked.

"Of course not," said Contessa. "I don't have the clearance for those kinds of details. Can you tell her to come get Sonny when you see her? This kid is driving me nuts."

Groober smiled. "I'll let her know."

\* \* \*

Harmonica and Miranda frowned at a brown patch of ferns.

"It used to be so pretty here," Miranda said.

"Get used to it," said Harmonica. "That's going to be all of the food in our garden."

"You can water the garden," Miranda said. "I included that in my calculations because I figured you would anyway. I only brought it up so Harvey would know you were serious."

"Really? Nice," Harmonica said.

Taddle Bill slid down the reservoir wall like his feet were covered in grease.

"Taddle, you're back," Harmonica said.

"Where's Harvey?" Taddle demanded.

"With Granny," said Harmonica. "How's the—"

"Move," Taddle said. He shoved his way past.

Harmonica scoffed. "Rude."

"And unforeseen," Miranda said. "Another delay in all likelihood. Don't worry. I'm sure Harvey saw it coming."

"Harmonica," Groober squeaked out from the top of the basin. It was all he could say. His lungs burned like a Joshua tree.

"Groober!" Harmonica said. "You're back too?"

"Here we go," Miranda said, crossing her arms.

Groober skidded down on his bottom and doddered over. "Harmonica," he said. He cleared his throat and added, "Miranda."

"Groober," Miranda said, over-enunciating.

"Was Taddle here?" Groober said.

"Yeah," said Harmonica. "You just missed him."

"Where is he now?" Groober asked.

"Looking for Harvey," said Harmonica. "Harvey is talking to Granny. I imagine that's where he went."

"Good," Groober said. He grabbed Harmonica's wrist. "I need your help."

Harmonica didn't move. "I can't, Groober. I have to pick up Sonny."

"This is an emergency," said Groober. "And I literally just checked on him. He and Contessa are fine. Can we go?"

"Okay, sure," Harmonica said.

"Thank you," said Groober. He nodded. "Good day, Miranda."

"Mm-hmm," Miranda replied.

* * *

Penny Plates stopped Taddle Bill atop a spiral stone staircase. Behind her, stalactites and stalagmites dueled like incisors at the mouth of Granny Pacquiao's cave.

"Where do you think you're going?" Penny asked.

"I need to talk to Harvey," said Taddle.

"He's with Granny," Penny said. "Whoever you're telling on is going to have to wait."

"This can't wait," Taddle said. He tried to bulldoze her, but Penny was thick as a brick wall. "Please move," Taddle continued. "It's very important."

"Take a seat if you'd like," said Penny. "I'll call your number when Harvey's ready."

Taddle tightened the grip on his shovel. Penny rigidified her stare.

"That I would love to see you try," Penny said.

Taddle sagged his shoulders and put his shovel down. Penny relaxed. Taddle juked to one side and broke to the other. Penny hooked his arm and hip-tossed him to the ground.

"That's it. I tried to play nice," Penny said. She patted her elbow and plopped on top of him. Taddle whimpered.

* * *

"We'll be all right, my behind," Anna said. She stood with Brute in front of Groober's teepee, blocking the entrance from view. "I'll be all right. You'd run like a Heterodontosaurus."

"No way," Brute said. "Groober can run much farther and faster than me."

Harmonica came up to join them. "Wow, this has to be serious if all of you are here."

"Groober didn't fill you in?" said Brute.

Groober ran a sweaty palm through his quills. "I, uh, didn't want to freak her out."

"Oh, geez," said Harmonica. "Should I freak out?"

"You shouldn't," Anna said. "But you might."

Brute dropped a mitt on Harmonica's shoulder. "Please promise me you won't freak out."

"Do I have to?" Harmonica said.

"Yes."

"Whatever. I promise."

"You promise what?"

"I promise I won't freak out."

"You promised. Remember that," Brute said. He stepped aside. "Take a peek."

Anna moved over. Harmonica gulped and pulled back the curtain. Her chest tightened, and she laughed like a woodpecker.

"She's going to freak out," Anna said.

Terror seized Harmonica's central nervous system. Brute clamped his paw over her mouth. A bloodcurdling shriek exploded from her crest. Half-deaf, Brute capped that as well.

"What about our promise?" Brute said. Harmonica breathed heavily through her nostrils. "I'm going to let go now," Brute continued. He uncovered Harmonica's mouth.

An elderly iguanodon exited the third teepee on the left. Anna smiled and waved. The iguanodon stared, turned his head, and went the other way.

Harmonica stuttered. "There's a C-Carnie in there."

"Relax," Brute said. "We p-put him there."

Harmonica slugged Brute's shoulder. "Why did you do that?" she said.

"Great question," said Brute. He rubbed his arm. "You want to take that one, Groob?"

"He needs your help," Groober said. "He's severely dehydrated, has second-degree sunburn over the majority of his body, and he's got gunk and stuff leaking from the back of his head."

"So," Harmonica said. "Why would I help him?"

"He's my friend," said Groober. "And if the roles were reversed, he'd be asking you to help me."

Harmonica massaged her temples. "This can't be real. I have to be dreaming."

"Want me to pinch you?" Anna said.

"It might take more than a pinch," said Harmonica. She fanned her face. "What do you think I should do?"

"Whatever you're comfortable with," Anna said.

"Nothing about this makes me feel comfortable," said Harmonica.

"Then do what you'll regret the least," said Anna.

"Right," said Harmonica. She took a deep breath and slapped Groober across the face.

"Ouch. What was that?" Groober said.

"The thing I'm going to regret the least," Harmonica said. She poked Groober's cheek. "Consider it a down payment. You owe me big for this."

"It's a blank check," Groober said. "Take it. It's yours."

"Don't worry," said Brute. "If anything happens, Anna and I are right here."

Harmonica nodded and leaned into the tent. She cradled Dino Mike's neck and lifted his head. His lips were chapped and covered with scabs. The size of his knot and the color of his goop made Harmonica wince. She set him down and reached backward. Brute grabbed her arm and pulled her to safety.

"Well?" Groober said.

"He's in bad shape," said Harmonica. "I can help, I think. But we need to move him to my shelter, and I mean stat."

\* \* \*

Taddle Bill crawled to his feet. Penny put up her dukes.

"You want to go another round?" Penny asked.

"Enough," said Taddle. "There's a Carnie in the Great Lands."

Penny dropped her fists and stared blankly. Taddle walked past and entered Granny's cave. Harvey's voice cracked like a whip.

"What?"

Harvey and Taddle ran out. Harvey backhanded a stalactite with a fist.

* * *

Anna grinned outside Groober's teepee.

"Taddle, welcome back," Anna said. "Harvey, Penny, good to see you both."

Harvey pushed Anna aside and swung his spiked tail, tearing Groober's teepee to shreds. It was empty. "Where is it?" Harvey demanded.

"I'm sorry," Anna said. "Where's what?"

* * *

Brute laid Dino Mike under the awning of Harmonica's lean-to, a sprawling pergola with vine-covered trellises built against a rock wall. Harmonica passed Groober a coconut full of water and ground some herbs in a tiny stone bowl. Groober took a sip. Harmonica smacked his hand.

"For him," Harmonica said. "Hold his head and pour it over his lips."

Abashed, Groober did as he was told. Water spilled everywhere. Harmonica took the coconut away and laid Dino Mike's head in her lap.

"I hope this helps." She smeared a slimy, green ointment over his lump, pried his jaws open, and poured water into his mouth.

"Any sign of Harvey?" Groober asked.

"Not yet," said Brute.

Harmonica touched Dino Mike's lips. "Poor guy. Someone grab me one of those aloe leaves and slice it in half."

"Got it," Groober said. He snapped a saw-toothed leaf off a plant in the corner.

Harmonica looked back down. Dino Mike's eyes were open. Harmonica gasped.

"Are you an angel?" Dino Mike said. "Did the allosaurus eat me?"

"Mr. Deinonychus!" Groober shouted. He dropped the aloe leaf and launched himself at Mike, accidentally stabbing him with his quills.

"Ow!" Dino Mike yelled. He gave Groober a weak shove and doubled over in pain.

"Oops. Sorry," Groober said.

"Groober?" said Dino Mike. His face puckered with sadness. "Did you die too?"

"Quite the contrary," said Groober. "Thanks to you, we're both very much alive."

"That doesn't make sense," Dino Mike said. His head pounded, but he sat up to take a look around. Brute lifted his tail.

"Where am I?" Dino Mike asked. "Who are they?"

Harmonica motioned for Brute to lower his weapon. "It's okay," Harmonica said. "He's not going to hurt us." She grabbed Dino Mike's hand. "You saved Groober's life. That makes all of us friends."

"If you say so," Dino Mike said. He grimaced and grabbed his lump. Harmonica slapped his hand.

"Nuh-uh," said Harmonica. "No touch, or no heal. Groober, where you at with that aloe?"

"Oh yeah," said Groober. "I have it right—"

Groober reached for the aloe. A humongous hoof squashed it from above. Groober trembled and craned his neck. "Harvey," he said.

"Hello, Groober," said Harvey.

"Is he a friend too?" Dino Mike asked.

"Shut it, Carnie," Harvey said. "You don't have any friends."

CHAPTER NINE
# MICHAEL DEINONYCHUS'S LAST MEAL

"Harvey," Harmonica said.

That's all she said. Harvey hushed her with a zip-it hand gesture. Penny and Taddle stood at Harvey's back, ready to cosign whatever he said. Anna mouthed Harmonica a silent apology.

"Let's get this over with," Harvey said. "Cooperate, and I'll make it quick and painless."

"Of course I will," said Dino Mike. Dehydration had rendered him delirious.

Harvey nodded. Penny lifted Dino Mike from behind. He tried to kick free, but Penny's grasp was firm.

"Be careful. He's injured," Harmonica said.

"That's a funny thing to tell the executioner," said Harvey.

"You don't want to do that, Harvey," Groober said. "Hear me out."

"That won't be necessary," said Harvey. He head-faked Groober, spun around him, and pointed out a stump. "That'll do." Penny threw Dino Mike down. "Taddle," Harvey continued, "break out Corrine."

Taddle Bill presented Harvey with a stone battle-axe. It had an edge like a box cutter and a wooden handle longer than Taddle's tail. Harvey spit in his palm and took Corrine in his possession. Dino Mike wrung his hands. His puny neck didn't stand a chance.

Harmonica wedged herself between Mike and Harvey. "Why won't you listen to Groober?" she demanded. "He said he has something to say."

"Taddle already filled me in," Harvey replied.

"He wasn't the only one out there," Harmonica said.

"That's what I said," said Anna. "He ignored me, flat-out."

Brute stepped forward. "There's more to the story here, Harv. It ain't gonna hurt nothing to let Groober talk."

Harvey suspired. "You have thirty seconds, Spinx. Only ten are left."

"This Carnie saved my life," Groober said.

"Don't care," said Harvey.

"He doesn't eat other dinosaurs."

"Don't believe you. Also, don't care."

"He can create fire."

"Good one," Harvey said. "Does he have a rain dance too?" He flexed his muscles at Harmonica. "Time's up. Move, or I will have you moved."

"That wasn't a lie," Harmonica said. "He's telling the truth."

"Nobody can create fire," Harvey said. "It only happens in, like, nature and stuff."

"There was definitely a fire," Brute said. "That's how we found them. We saw the smoke all the way from the water tree."

"Did you see the Carnie start it?" Harvey asked.

"No," said Brute.

"I did," Groober said.

"I believe him," said Anna. "If Groober says the Carnie started the fire, the Carnie started the fire. He also said the Carnie used it to scare off an allosaurus."

"That's insane," Harvey said. He turned back to Harmonica and narrowed his stare. "I'm not asking again."

"I'm not going anywhere," said Harmonica. "This isn't your decision to make. This goes above you."

"Please," Harvey scoffed. "Nobody cares what that old fossil thinks." He glanced at Taddle from the corner of his eye. Taddle railroaded Harmonica out of the way.

"Harvey, stop it!" Harmonica exclaimed.

Penny pressed down on Dino Mike's shoulders, knocking him windless. Harvey swung back his axe. Dino Mike squeezed his eyes shut. He felt a whoosh of air, but the axe never came down. Mike opened an eyelid. Brute held Harvey's axe by the handle just beneath the head.

"Nobody disrespects Granny," Brute said. "Not even you." He and Harvey locked eyes. A conch horn blew in the distance.

"Fine," Harvey said. "Invite the Carnie to supper and incite mass panic. That way, you can hear the order come from her mouth instead of mine." He wrested the axe from Brute and tossed it to Taddle, who let go of Harmonica to make a clumsy catch. Harmonica shoved him.

"Don't ever touch me again," she said.

"What should I do?" Penny asked. Dino Mike looked like a rug compressed beneath her weight.

"Make sure our guest arrives on time," said Harvey. He strode away.

Anna narrowed her eyes as Penny lightened the load on Dino Mike's back. Harmonica knelt beside him with pity.

"Are you okay?" Harmonica said.

"Is my neck still attached to my body?" Dino Mike asked.

"For now." Harmonica smiled nervously.

"You don't think it's going to stay that way?" Dino Mike said.

Harmonica shrugged. "That's up to Granny. Whatever she says goes."

Dino Mike chuckled. Nobody else laughed. He cleared his throat. "She can't be worse than that guy?"

"She's a stone-cold Carnie killer, bro," Brute said. "Harvey ain't got nothing on Granny."

Dino Mike gulped. Groober tapped the tips of his claws. Harmonica rubbed Dino Mike's shoulder.

"Do you have that aloe, Groober?" Harmonica asked.

\* \* \*

The prongs of a forked path converged toward a massive stony clearing. Four long tables ran the length of the tract. A fifth, V-shaped table was elevated front and center. Behind it sat an impressive wooden throne. These were the supper grounds, and dozens of Herbies of all shapes and sizes filed in, forming a lunch line along an organic stone wall.

Contessa Treehorn dipped a scoop in a crate and heaped a mound of olive du jour onto a waiting victim's plate. The Herbie on the receiving end scowled.

"Next!" Contessa shouted.

The Herbies shifted. The elderly iguanodon from three teepees down moved to the front of the line.

"Olives?" the iguanodon whined.

"Don't start with me, Norm," Contessa said. "Today ain't the day."

Behind Norm came bustling and groaning.

"Excuse me. Pardon me. Watch it, hot coffee coming through." Harvey Plates swam through the Herbies. Miranda McBeek blocked his path.

"Harvey," Miranda said. "How'd it go with Granny?"

"Tremendous, absolutely tremendous," Harvey said impatiently.

"Are we putting the conservation measures in place?" said Miranda.

"We'll speak on that in a bit," said Harvey. He used his forearm like a windshield wiper and swiped Miranda away. Harvey cut past Norm, sank a grubby hook into Contessa's crate, and shoveled a fistful of olives into his mouth. Contessa bopped him with her scoop.

"Gross, Harvey. There's a line here, if you didn't notice."

"Like I'd wait in line for something you cooked," said Harvey. He faced the grumbling crowd and cleared his throat. "Everybody, listen up. This is a matter of herd security. I need you all to take your seats immediately."

"What about our places in line?" Norm asked.

"That's not important right now," Harvey said. "The only thing that matters to me is your safety. To ensure that, I'm asking you all to please take your seats and await further instruction."

"What's going on?" Contessa whispered. "This doesn't have anything to do with—"

"Harmonica!" Sonny shouted. He squirted out from behind a stack of crates, shot through the cafeteria, and latched on to Harmonica's leg. "Contessa says you're late."

"I'm sorry," Harmonica said. Contessa glared from her stonewall service station. "Groober said he spoke with her." Groober fiddled with his fingers.

Sonny tugged on Harmonica's arm and whispered in her ear. "She's mean, and she yells," he said. "Please don't leave me with her again."

A nervous energy channeled through the crowd. Herbies whispered and turned their heads as Brute and Penny ushered Dino Mike up the center aisle between tables. They, along with Anna and Taddle, stopped before the head table.

"Aw, who's this little guy?" Dino Mike said. Sonny lowered his head, planted his foot, and plowed into Mike's shin with six inches of bone-crushing skull. Dino Mike yelped.

"Sonny!" said Harmonica. She pulled him back by the tail.

"What?" Sonny said. "It's a Carnie."

Dino Mike hobbled and flexed his leg. Sonny reared back, growled, and revved his engine.

"Sonny, no," Harmonica said. "Wait with Contessa." Sonny puffed his chest to argue. Harmonica pointed sternly. "Go."

Sonny deflated and slogged back to Contessa, mean-mugging Dino Mike the entire way. Contessa rewarded Sonny with a slick high five.

"Cute kid," Dino Mike muttered. The supper grounds stirred. Those who were seated stood. "What's going on?" Dino Mike asked.

"Quiet," Harmonica said. "Granny's coming. Stand tall. She doesn't like slouchers."

Dino Mike straightened his back.

*Click. Tick. Tack.* A gnarled walking stick percussed the rocky desert pavement. Granny Pacquiao, an ancient Pachycephalosaurus with an eye patch and a cracked, bony crown, descended her stone staircase. With one deliberate step after another, she made her way toward the throne. Harvey Plates straightened his shoulders and pulled out Granny's chair. Granny glanced down at Dino Mike.

"This ought to be good," Granny said. She sat. Harvey scooted her in. With a faint wave of her hand, she coaxed everyone present to park it as well.

"Grandmother," Harvey said. "Before we eat, we've urgent matters to discuss."

"Does this have anything to do with that Carnie?" Granny snarked.

"It does," said Harvey.

"Spit it out," said Granny. "I haven't got all night."

"Right," said Harvey. "The crew at the water tree found the Carnie unconscious in the Bad Lands.

For some reason, they brought it back here to see what they should do with it. I ordered its execution on sight."

"He's alive," Granny said. "I'm staring right at him." The Herbies laughed like a live studio audience.

"The thing is, some insisted I bring the final decision to you," said Harvey.

"Why someone would question your judgment is beyond me," said Granny.

"Thank you, Grandmother," Harvey said. Oblivious to her sarcasm, he walked around the table and snatched his battle-axe from Taddle. "If it pleases you, I can close this case right now."

Granny waved him off. "Not here. You'll spoil my supper."

"Right," Harvey said. He made Taddle take the axe back. "After we eat, then."

"Perhaps," Granny said. She dissected Dino Mike with her good eye. Mike wasn't sure if he'd turned to stone or not. "Why would somebody want to keep you alive?"

Harmonica cleared her throat. "Grandmother, if I may?"

"I should've known," Granny said. She rolled her eye. "Let's hear it. While I'm young."

"I asked Harvey to bring this before you because I feel like the circumstances we're dealing with are unique," Harmonica said. "I'm confident once you hear Groober's side, you'll agree we can arrive at a more amicable solution."

"Why are you talking if he's the one with the story?" Granny said.

Groober's mouth quivered. His eyes darted between Granny and Dino Mike. Granny exaggerated a sigh. Harmonica kicked the back of Groober's knee.

"Gran, *ahem*, Grandmother," Groober said. "The first point I'd like to . . . point out . . . is I wouldn't be alive if it wasn't for Dino Mike."

"The Carnie?" Granny said.

"Yes, the Carnie," said Groober. "His name is Mi—"

"I didn't ask for his name," Granny said. "Why is he here?"

"Because he needed our help," Groober said. "He was bloodied, concussed, sunburnt, and dehydrated. If we didn't bring him here, he would have died. You're going to ask me why you should care."

"Took the words right out of my mouth," said Granny.

"You should care because he sustained the bulk of those injuries saving my life from a bloodthirsty allosaurus," Groober said. The crowd shared a gasp.

Granny rapped her knuckles on the table. From her point of view, Dino Mike looked like a used pipe cleaner. "I'm having a really hard time picturing it," Granny said.

"I'm not," said Harvey. "It looks just like it sounds. Like a steaming pile of dung."

"He used fire," Groober said. "Fire he created. He scared the allosaurus away."

Somewhere in the supper grounds, a horsefly sneezed. Granny leaned forward, and her eye pierced Dino Mike's soul. "Is it true?" Granny asked.

"Which part?" said Dino Mike.

"All of it," said Granny. "Did you create fire and scare an allosaurus away?"

"I started the fire, yeah," said Dino Mike. "The rest of it is a little fuzzy, to be honest."

"Could you do it again?"

"What? Start a fire? No."

"What if your life depended on it?"

"I mean, technically," Dino Mike said. "But I won't."

"You got that axe handy, Harvey?" said Granny.

Harvey grabbed Corrine so fast he peeled a layer of prints from Taddle Bill's fingers. "Just give me the word," he said.

Granny propped her elbows on the table and smirked at Dino Mike. "Last chance. Is that your final answer?"

"I'm sorry," Dino Mike said. "It has to be a hard no. If I start a fire, everything you've built will burn to the ground. Trust me, I've seen it happen twice. It isn't safe."

"What do you care about our safety?" said Granny.

"I didn't come here to harm you," said Dino Mike.

"You don't want to eat us?" Granny said.

"Not even a little bit," said Dino Mike. "I don't eat other dinosaurs."

Granny rapped her knuckles again and turned to Groober. "Is that true?"

"The only thing I've ever seen him eat was a bite of Hedera," Groober said. "Honestly."

"Vegetables?" Granny asked.

The Herbies chattered like teeth. Dino Mike's blood froze. Groober's words were based in fact, but they left out the part where Dino Mike puked.

"You eat vegetables?" Granny said.

"I mean, not just vegetables," said Dino Mike. "I eat fish and mammals and stuff." He counted on his hand. "Birds. Centipedes. Scorpions."

"Enough," said Harvey. "He's a Carnie. He doesn't eat vegetables."

"Does too," Groober said.

"We'll see about that," Harvey said. He put his axe down, picked up a plate of olives, and forced a handful into Dino Mike's mouth. Groober's eyes popped out of his sockets.

"If he keeps those down, I'll be his date to the meteor shower," Harvey said.

The olives were warm, waxy, and bitter. They beckoned Dino Mike to blow chunks, but he clamped down and fought to hold them in. Thinking about how much he detested Harvey didn't seem to help. He tried pretending the olives were eggs, but that didn't work either. They were that disgusting. With watery eyes, Dino Mike thought about his nieces. He pictured them fighting over a hummingbird and forced himself to swallow. Bile and rancor danced in his throat. Harvey beamed with anticipation. Groober searched for places to run. Dino Mike uncovered his mouth.

"He's going to blow," Anna whispered.

"*Brraaaaapppp!*"

That was it. No olives, not a single pith or pit. Just one tectonic belch.

"Excuse me," Dino Mike said. He wiped his mouth. He was as shocked as everyone, except maybe Groober, who was drenched in an icy sweat.

"Well, I'll be," Granny said. "Harvey found himself a date."

The Herbies lost it. Harmonica belted out laughter. Dino Mike smiled. Granny rocked in her chair.

"I'm going to ask this once," Granny said. "Why did you come here?"

Every ear in the supper grounds was aimed at Dino Mike. He drew a breath and said, "I came to invite you to come back to the Good Lands. Things are different now."

Granny stopped rocking. Groober's stock in Dino Mike crashed. Harvey reached for the axe, but Granny held up a hand.

"You've wasted your time," Granny said.

"No, really," said Dino Mike. "We've changed. No one is going to eat you. You shouldn't have to live out here without food or water."

"We're not coming back," Granny said. "Who else knows about us?"

"No one," Dino Mike said. "I followed Groober here by myself. It's only me, I swear."

"You haven't lied to me yet," Granny said. "At least I don't think you have, which is more than I can say about most of the dinosaurs here. If I let you go, are you going to tell your friends about us?"

"Not a soul," Dino Mike said. "I promise."

Harvey twirled his axe. "We are not letting this Carnie walk out of here alive."

"Sit down, Harvey, or I'll send you back with him," Granny bellowed. She pondered for a moment. "Ms. Anthophilous?"

"Yes, Grandmother?" Harmonica said.

"How long until our friend here will be strong enough to travel?"

"Two or three days, maybe. If he staves off infection."

"The meteor shower is two nights away," Granny said. "I trust you'll keep an eye on him until then."

"Of course," Harmonica said.

Harvey pounded his fist. "This is where we sleep."

"Sleep well knowing you're safe from allosauri," Granny said. "If you need to worry about something, worry about our water arriving on time. Is this delay going to affect anything?"

"Of course not," Harvey said. "We have plenty of water as is, and the team's heading back out to finish after supper. I'll even send Penny with them to make up for lost time."

"Very well," said Granny. "If it's all settled, then, what are we waiting for? Someone get me a plate of olives. I'm starving over here."

In the middle of the crowd, Miranda McBeek's eyes turned a murderous shade of red.

CHAPTER TEN
# DANCING TO HARMONICA'S TUNE

A hefty tree trunk served as a drill bit with a chiseled, granite tip. It climbed the hollow core of a wooden derrick, pausing at its peak. A bamboo cable went slack, and the hunk of wood plummeted, disappearing down a wormhole with a diameter barely wider than its own.

*Ka-chunk!*

Penny Plates wiped her sweaty brow. The sunrise cast an antique filter over the rickety, timber tower, which, at forty or so feet tall, was dwarfed by its companion, a mighty, hundred-foot cottonwood, the Herbies' beloved water tree. To the west, two king-size supply canopies housed nets full of olives, spare palm leaves, and buckets of tar.

The water tree was ancient and elephantine. Wrinkled gray bark peeled from its trunk like wallpaper, biological evidence of its century-long existence. Miraculously, the cottonwood still sprouted leaves and bore shattered fruit, not on all of its branches, but some. This raised a huge question. *Where did it get its water?*

Penny tramped over to the derrick and picked up the loose end of the cable. She wrapped it around her wrist, threw it over her shoulder, and walked the other way, raising the drill bit for another go.

*Ka-chunk!*

Brute Grimstone nibbled the tip of a palm leaf. He stood in the middle of a trench as deep and as wide as he was tall. Sweat beaded on his forehead. Piles of dirt and hollow logs lined the top of the ditch. Carefully, Brute lowered the end of a twenty-foot trunk and lined it up with the back side of another. Taddle Bill pushed with all his weight. The makeshift pipes clicked together, linking to a dozen or so others and a hand-dug basin at the foot of the derrick.

Brute stood and stretched his aching back. "How far we got to go?" he asked.

Panting, Taddle turned his head. He slouched. The channel outran his vision. "You don't want to know."

Outside the trench, a fat desert termite danced along the ledge of a hollow log at the top of a pyramid. Anna dug her heels in the dirt and shoved the log off. It raced toward Brute and Taddle.

"Coming in hot!" Anna shouted.

Brute's mouth fell open. The palm leaf dropped. Centrifugal force glued the termite to the rolling palm's walls. Brute and Taddle held their arms up and braced for impact. The log crashed into them. The termite flew through empty space and smacked against the other side.

"Watch it," Taddle said. "You're going to bust a pipe."

"I'm sorry," Anna replied saucily. "That one got away from me a little."

Brute and Taddle lowered the pipe into the trench. The dizzy termite reached a wobbly foot out, touched solid ground, and willed its thorax to follow. Brute lined the log up. Taddle clicked it into place. The three of them—Brute, Taddle, and the termite—all exhaled heavily.

"How far we got to go?" Brute asked. Taddle Bill frowned.

"Think fast!" Anna said. She sent another pipe screaming from the top of the pile. Brute and Taddle jump-spun around. Brute's hoof stamped the termite into paste.

*Ka-chunk!*

\* \* \*

On the outskirts of the Great Lands, Harvey Plates sank his battle-axe into the side of a tree. It was early, but he had sweat-stained pits. Behind him, Norm and three other miserable iguanodons dug a ditch against their will.

In the olive grove, Dino Mike yawned and stretched his jaws, but his eyelids stayed droopy. Sonny held Eggbert like a watermelon and kept his gaze on Mike.

"What's with the kid?" Dino Mike asked.

"Sonny?" Harmonica said. She was perched in an olive tree. "He's Granny's grandson. She has trouble keeping up with him sometimes, so I watch him during the day."

"No, I get it, but why does he keep looking at me like that?"

Harmonica dropped a bushel of olives onto a net. "You're a Carnie. What do you expect?"

"I don't know," said Dino Mike. "He's a kid. Why doesn't he go play or something?"

"He doesn't have anyone to play with. Other than Eggbert."

"The egg has a name?" Dino Mike said. His stomach wailed. He hunched to suppress it.

"What egg doesn't?" said Harmonica.

"We don't usually name ours. Not until they hatch, anyway." Mike nodded at Sonny. "You know, I used to eggsit for my sister. There are ways to have fun doing it."

"Your sister has eggs?" Harmonica said.

"Had," said Dino Mike. "They've hatched."

"Aww," said Harmonica. "Males or females?"

"Females," Dino Mike said. "Ash and Fern. My two beautiful nieces."

"How sweet," said Harmonica. "It had to be tough leaving them behind."

Dino Mike's smile faded. "Hey, Sonny. You know the main thing I used to do when I was watching eggs?"

"Eat them?" Sonny said.

"Sonny!" said Harmonica. She hit him in the neck with an olive.

Dino Mike chuckled. "It's okay. No, I didn't eat them. But I did dance. A lot."

"Whatever," said Sonny.

"What's wrong?" Dino Mike asked. He twisted his ankles and his knees. "Afraid I'll make you look bad?"

"How can you dance?" Sonny said. "There isn't any music."

"That's the great thing about music," said Dino Mike. He picked up a clump of olives and shook it like a maraca. "It's hiding all around you."

Naturally, Sonny bobbed his head.

"There you go," Dino Mike said. "Do you want to try?" He tossed the olives. Sonny leaned back. The maraca hit the ground and Dino Mike frowned. "I think we've had a breakdown in communication."

"Maybe I can help," Harmonica said. She took a deep breath and hummed. A sumptuous ballad poured from her crest. Goose bumps covered Dino Mike's arms and his pupils dilated, blacking out his irises. Harmonica blushed.

"Why did you stop?" Dino Mike asked. "That was incredible."

"Well, it's hard to play when you're staring like that," said Harmonica.

"My fault," Dino Mike said. He covered his eyes. "Please, proceed."

Harmonica smiled. "Fine," she said. "But only if Sonny says it's okay."

Dino Mike clasped his hands and begged. Sonny rolled his eyes. "Yeah, whatever."

Dino Mike pumped his fist. "Yes!"

Harmonica grinned, cleared her throat, and hammered out an upbeat, funky tune.

"Oh yeah," Dino Mike said, dancing. "Yeah. That's my jam." He bobbed and pivoted, transitioning into a wonky running dinosaur. "Step back, Sonny, you don't want none of this."

Sonny cracked a smile. Harmonica almost fell out of her tree. "Okay, calm down," she said with a giggle. "You're supposed to be healing, remember?"

"What's wrong?" Dino Mike said. "You don't like my moves?"

"I just don't want Harvey to see you and think you're conjuring evil spirits. He's already building a wall to keep the rest of the Carnies out. Do you really want to test him?"

"Fine," Dino Mike said. "I have a better idea anyway." He scooped up a pair of rocks. Sonny lowered his head.

"Sonny James Pacquiao!" Harmonica shouted.

"I'm sorry," Sonny said. "I don't trust him."

"I accept that," said Dino Mike. "I just want to play a game. You ever kicked rocks?"

"That doesn't sound like a game," said Sonny.

"It is," Dino Mike said. "In fact, it's the very best game I know."

"I don't want to play," said Sonny.

"You don't even know how," said Dino Mike. He stepped in front of a tree, drew a line in the dirt, and placed the rocks behind it. "Now what you do is—"

"Kick the rocks?"

"Exactly. It's not that simple though. There are two trees, the home tree and the mid-tree. We alternate kicks. The first one to go down, kick their rock off the mid-tree, come back, and kick it off the home tree wins."

"Sounds easy."

"Here's where it gets hairy," Dino Mike said. "Say you kick your rock, then I kick mine and hit yours. I get to choose if I want to kick my rock again or kick yours as far as I want in any direction."

"What's so hairy about that?" Sonny asked.

"I guess you'll have to wait and see. You playing, Harmonica?"

"No thanks. Somebody has to get some work done around here."

"That's right, I forgot," said Dino Mike. "Would you rather we helped?"

"I think you're going to need more help than me," said Harmonica.

"Right," Dino Mike said. He waved at Sonny. "You want to go first?"

"No, you go," Sonny said.

"Fine. Watch and learn." Dino Mike let it rip at three-quarters speed. The rock bounced and rolled. Sonny snorted. "What? You think you can do better?" Dino Mike asked.

"I can't do any worse," said Sonny. He lined up his toe and took eight paces back.

"Don't overthink things," Dino Mike said. "A run-up could really affect your accuracy."

Sonny ignored Mike's advice and ran into his kick. The rock shot off his foot like a laser. It nicked Dino Mike's rock and rolled several yards past.

"Maybe I can be as good as you one day," Sonny said.

"Beginner's luck," said Dino Mike. "Go ahead. You get to kick again."

"I thought I could kick yours?"

"You could. But with a turn like that, the smart thing to do would be—"

Sonny booted Dino Mike's rock. It sailed down over the ledge and into the reservoir. The water rippled. Harmonica clapped and hollered.

"Woo-hoo!" Harmonica said. "Sign him up. The kid is a natural."

\* \* \*

Contessa lay on a palm leaf pillow and bathed in the sun. A pair of round pebbles, painted like eyeballs, covered her peepers.

"Hey, Contessa," Harmonica said. She hauled two olive nets, one over each shoulder. Behind her, Dino Mike's knees buckled under the weight of one.

"Harmonica," Contessa said, removing her pebbles. "How are you, sweetie?"

"Another day away from paradise," said Harmonica. She dropped her nets, grabbed Dino Mike's, and threw it on the pile. Dino Mike breathed a sigh of relief.

"Di-no Mike," Contessa said, dragging out the first couple syllables to express her affection. "How are you doing, baby? Harmonica isn't overworking you, is she?"

"Her? No way," Dino Mike said. "She's easy. It's Sonny who gave me my beating."

"That boy's a handful," said Contessa. Sonny yawned at Harmonica's side. "Looks like you're not the only one who's worn out."

Sonny hid. Dino Mike admired Contessa's kitchen. "Nice setup you got here. Is this where the magic happens?"

"This is where the supper happens," said Contessa.

"How does it all work?" Dino Mike asked. "What's your secret?"

"Nothing crazy," Contessa said. "I spread the olives out on the hot rock to soak up some vitamin D. I hit 'em with a shimmy of this and a sham of that, and voilà, everyone complains."

"I don't know what they're griping about," said Dino Mike. "Those were literally the best olives I've ever had."

Contessa blushed. "Why, thank you, Dino Mike. That's so nice of you to say."

"We've got to get going," Harmonica said. "Got to see what Groober brought me back from the Good Lands. I'm taking Michael to see the garden."

Dino Mike cringed. "Ugh. The unabridged version."

"What? Michael?" said Harmonica. "It's a strong name. What's wrong with it?"

"Nothing," Dino Mike said. "If you want to sound like my sister."

Harmonica waved Dino Mike off. Sonny tugged on Harmonica's arm.

"I'm tired," Sonny whispered. "Can I stay here?"

Harmonica raised her eyebrows and smiled. Contessa frowned.

"He must have worn his little legs out kicking my butt," Dino Mike said. Harmonica snorted and covered her mouth.

"You know what? It's fine," Contessa said. "I'll take the rascal for a while. But if he gets ornery, I'm hunting you down."

"Thanks so much, Contessa," Harmonica said. "I think he's ready for a nap, anyway."

"You're ready for a nap," said Dino Mike. Harmonica punched him in the arm.

* * *

Groober Spinx's feet stuck out from the ramshackle canopy he'd salvaged from his Harvey-Plates-ravaged home. Harmonica kicked him.

"Are you really still in bed?" Harmonica said.

"Ugh," Groober grumbled. "What time is it?"

"Midafternoon," said Harmonica.

"Come back when it's closer to midevening," said Groober. "I should be up by then." He curled into a fetal position.

Harmonica dropped to her belly and flashed a fluorescent smile. "Michael and I were on our way to the garden."

Dino Mike rolled his eyes. "Again with the standard issue."

"Shut it," said Harmonica. "Anywho, we were dropping by to see if you brought any seeds or bulbs back from the Good Lands."

"I guess Michael didn't tell you," Groober said.

"Tell me what exactly?" said Harmonica. Dino Mike shrugged.

"He torched my seeds and specimens," said Groober. "All of them."

"I most certainly did not," said Dino Mike.

"Did too," said Groober. "They were in my coat."

"Oh," Dino Mike said. He grimaced. "I guess I did then. But not on purpose, I swear."

Harmonica pushed herself up and knocked the dirt off her thighs. "It's not your fault," she said. "You were under attack. We shouldn't be using the extra water anyway. C'mon, I'll show you what we've already planted for now."

"Cool," Dino Mike said. "Nice catching up with you, Groober."

"Hold up a sec," Groober said. Squinty-eyed and scanty-tailed, he rolled out of his tent and grabbed Dino Mike's wrist. "Could I speak with Michael alone for a moment?"

"No problem," Harmonica said. "I'll just be right over there."

Harmonica left the cul-de-sac. Groober let go of Mike's hand.

"What do you think you're doing?" Groober asked.

"Touring the garden," Dino Mike said. "What's with throwing me under the bus?"

"What's with the olive voodoo you pulled at supper last night?"

"I don't know how that happened. I thought I was going to puke for sure."

"Well, you didn't," said Groober. "And now everyone thinks you're some sort of superhero because you start fires and fight allosauri."

"Allosaurus. It was only one," Dino Mike said. "And I don't remember fighting him."

"I don't care. You need to leave. Tonight."

"But Granny said I can stay."

"Granny doesn't know you lied to her."

"You lied," Dino Mike said. "I gave her an alternate truth."

"You said the Carnies wouldn't eat us if we went back to the Good Lands," said Groober.

"And they won't," said Dino Mike.

"Is that so?" said Groober. "Because Harmonica misses the Good Lands more than anybody. She'd be the first to volunteer to go back, and you're saying the Carnies wouldn't touch her? What about Sonny? Do you even care?"

"I'm not sure what you're getting at," Dino Mike said.

"Are you really that dense?" said Groober. "You can't have your friends and eat them too."

"Groober."

"Don't Groober me. We are not friends. You saved my life. I saved yours. We're even. That's it."

"Technically, I saved your life twice," said Dino Mike. "But who's counting?"

"I'll give you one chance to leave and do what's right," said Groober. "If you're still here tomorrow, I have to do what's right."

"C'mon, Groober."

"Good day, Mr. Deinonychus," Groober said. He ducked and disappeared under his canopy. Dino Mike's face twitched.

\* \* \*

"We're almost there," Harmonica said giddily. "No peeking."

"How could I?" said Dino Mike. "Your hands are bigger than my head."

"Shush," said Harmonica. "I didn't want to spoil the surprise. We're here. Are you ready?"

"The anticipation's killing me," Dino Mike said. His nostrils puckered. "So is the smell. What is that? It's awful."

"It's, um . . . fertilizer," said Harmonica. "Don't worry, it goes away after a while. Anyway . . . one, two, three." She uncovered Dino Mike's eyes. "Ta-da! What do you think?"

"It looks like my new den," Dino Mike said. "There's nothing here but dirt."

Harmonica flicked the back of his skull. "Don't look with your eyes, dummy. Look with your heart."

Dino Mike plugged his nose. "Should I smell with my heart too?"

"I said you'd get used to it," Harmonica said. "C'mon. Let me show you around."

Harmonica dragged Dino Mike through freshly tilled soil and pointed to a row of baby sprouts. "Those are horsetails and cycads," she said. "We're growing different kinds of roots and berries over here. Oh, and that giant field over there? Nothing but humongous ferns."

"Is that where Groober's going to hide?"

"What?"

"Never mind."

"Back there, think oak, maple, and sycamore trees. They'll take a while to grow, but in time they'll tickle the sky and touch the horizon." Harmonica gripped Dino Mike's elbow. "This is my favorite part here. The flowers. I'm talking lilies, daisies, proteas, tulips, and magnolias. You name it, we got it."

"Flowers, huh? What's so special about them?"

"Aside from the obvious ecological advantages like attracting bees and butterflies?"

"Obviously," Dino Mike said.

"They make me happy," said Harmonica. "And they smell really nice, which helps to mask the dung."

"Dung?" Dino Mike said. He hopped on a boulder. "You said it was fertilizer."

"And what do you suppose fertilizer is, dummy?" Harmonica giggled and reclined next to Mike to take in the view. "You know, we really are doing the best we can out here. It's not the Good Lands, and it never will be, but it's all we have."

"You really miss it there, don't you?" Dino Mike said.

"The Good Lands is my home," said Harmonica. "Of course I miss it."

"What do you miss the most?"

"Psh. The food. The weather. Everything. The ocean tide rolling in and rinsing the sand from my body. You know what? The beach. That's what I miss the most, and that's something we'll never be able to replicate here. How about you? Do you miss it?"

"Huh?" Dino Mike said. "Yeah, I guess."

"That sounds convincing."

"I really miss my nieces."

"I'm sure they really miss you too," said Harmonica. "You're good with children. I've never seen Sonny warm up to someone so fast."

"I think it's cool that you take care of him," Dino Mike said. "Where are his parents?"

"Really?" Harmonica said.

"Did I say something wrong?" Dino Mike asked. "It was an honest question. I didn't mean any offense by it."

"They were eaten," Harmonica said. She ran her hand along a column of marching ants. "All of our parents were."

"I'm sorry," Dino Mike said. "I didn't know."

"You didn't know, or you didn't think about it?" said Harmonica. "Anyway, you don't have to be sorry. It's the way of the world, right? Or at least it's the way things used to be. The whole food chain, circle of life, et cetera."

"That doesn't make it okay," Dino Mike said. He flicked one ant, and the others fled for their lives.

Harmonica stared out into nothingness. "You know, Granny says this meteor shower only comes around every twenty years. It's dazzling, she says, like fire raining from the sky."

"Sounds incredible," Dino Mike said.

"Do you think you'd want to watch it with me?" Harmonica asked.

Dino Mike shifted and nearly slid off the boulder before regaining his composure. He cleared his throat. "Um, what?"

"If you can get out of your date with Harvey, that is," Harmonica said. "If not, no big deal."

Dino Mike's digits went fuzzy and numb. A conch horn blew in the distance.

## CHAPTER ELEVEN
# UNCLE SHANK

"Sit still," Betty said. She tried in vain to scrub a thick layer of dirt from the top of Fern's head. The look on Fern's face said it all. She loathed bath time, but Betty wasn't letting her get away without one. "How do you get so filthy?"

Ash giggled, waist-deep in the winding creek. Bath time was a treat for her. Seeing Fern struggle was a cherry on top. Fern didn't share her sense of humor. She slapped the water's surface and splashed Ash in the face.

"Fern!" Betty shouted. Fern shrugged like she'd done nothing wrong. "Go stand in the corner until we're done," Betty said.

Ash stuck out her tongue. Fern dunked her head in passing. Ash spit out water and shook out her feathers.

"At least one of you knows how to behave," Betty said. Her nose was chapped, and her tear ducts were swollen. Lines of melancholy mapped out her face. Ash latched on to Betty's leg.

A minnow shimmered like liquid mercury. Fern ran her tongue over her teeth and sank her jaws in the water. She came out with a mouthful of seaweed and a fresh coat of mud.

"Hey," somebody whispered. Fern glanced over. Bernadette's smile filled the space between the blades of a plant. Fern smiled back. How could she not? "Look how pretty you are," Bernadette continued. "Come here so I can get a better look at you."

Fern checked over her shoulder. Betty pampered Ash. Fern looked back. Bernadette coaxed her with open arms.

"That's it, baby. Come to Auntie Bernie."

Fern took a few steps and noticed Shrapnel twitching in the plant next door. Startled, she dug her heels in the mud and took a step back.

"No, no, no," Bernie said. "It's okay." She lifted Shrapnel by the feathers. "See? It's only my brother."

Shrapnel fidgeted and scratched his neck. "Can we eat her yet?"

"You fool," Hack said. He popped out of another plant and tried to snatch Fern, but she fell back, splashed, and barked for help. Betty was there in an instant.

"What's the matter?" Betty said. She scooped Fern up. "How did you get so dirty?"

Fern pointed a shaky claw. Betty parted the tall-bladed plant. The raptors were gone. Ash rubbed her sister's shoulders. Betty sniffed the air.

\* \* \*

"How far do you think we would have made it?" Delilah said. She braided two vines to keep her hands busy. Her malnourished fingers were basically bone. "Farther than Michael? Farther than Betty when she went looking for him?"

Odin hacked a low-hanging branch. He, too, had lost considerable weight. "I don't understand the question. We were never going anywhere."

"You know what I mean," said Delilah. "If you and Betty never had eggs, hypothetically speaking, and you and I ran away together. How far do you think we could have gone?"

"Aren't you forgetting about Shank?"

"Am I?" said Delilah. She stepped over her sky-gazing post and paused. "I always thought he and Betty would have been perfect for each other."

Betty appeared at the edge of the den. "Odin. We need to talk."

"I wasn't," Odin said. "I mean, I didn't. I don't. What?"

Moments later, Odin puffed his chest and paced in the den. Adrenaline coursed through his veins.

"Do you want to run that by me one more time?" Odin asked.

"Like I said. I was bathing Ash," said Betty. "Fern wandered off. She cried, and I came right over. There wasn't anyone there, but I smelled Carnie."

"Why weren't you watching her?" said Odin.

"I was right there," Betty said. "Pay attention. Focus on the issue."

"It sounds like an issue to me," said Odin. "I'm already down two hunters. Now I have to leave another behind because you're incapable of babysitting?"

"I don't babysit," Betty said. "I parent. You should try it."

"Gah," said Odin. "Where is Shank when I need him?"

* * *

A plump and ugly bullfrog spun across the face of the moon on the surface of a pond. Its vocal sack rose and fell to the rhythm of the night.

A stringy patch of seaweed skated across the water. A stream of air bubbles popped, and a crocodilian snout rose from the depths. Shank Nightcuss stood with a spear and nary a sound. Water rolled from his body as he locked on to his prey.

The spear whizzed by. The bullfrog licked a pupil and dove into the pond.

Shank crawled ashore like a swamp monster covered in sludge. He lashed out and tore an innocent bush to shreds. His rib cage rose in his chest. Shank bent to retrieve his spear but stood without grabbing it. His head tilted in awe. In a clearing, Poseidon snored on all fours like a cow. His head was pressed against the side of a tree.

Shank salivated over Poseidon's meaty thighs. It was too bad there wasn't a deinonychus alive bad enough to take him. Poseidon could've squashed Shank like a bug.

Shank grabbed his spear. A glob of seaweed dangled from its edge. Shank wrapped the weeds around his claws and pondered. A creepy smile crawled over his face.

* * *

Betty jolted free from a nightmare. Her feathers were clumped with sticky, cold sweat, and she didn't feel the warmth or weight of her children anywhere. She glanced at Dino Mike's bed. Ash slept under Odin's wing and out-snored her daddy. Betty smiled and strutted over to check on Fern. She wasn't there. Betty clawed Odin's rib.

"Odin!"

"Ouch. What do you want?" Odin said. Ash wiggled grumpily under his arm.

"Where's Fern?" Betty asked.

"She's right . . ." Odin trailed off. "She's not with you?"

\* \* \*

Fern moseyed through the jungle with a porous mind and wagging tail. She wasn't afraid of the dark or of being alone. Her night vision was crisp, and a host of fresh sights, flowers in particular, begged for her attention. She plunged her nose into every petal.

A moonbeam parted the treetops, capping an otherworldly red tulip with a glimmering, white halo. Fern zoned in, entranced by its beauty. She leaned and took a whiff. Something buzzed from the flower's center and landed on her snout. Fern's eyes went cross. A rugged dragonfly came into focus. Fern's tummy grumbled. She clamped her jaws, but the dragonfly whirred out of reach.

Fern licked her teeth and zigged. The dragonfly zagged. Fern followed and snapped, but she came up short again. Fed up, Fern crossed her arms and pouted. The dragonfly hovered closer. Fern pounced. The ground crumbled beneath her.

When the dust settled, Fern lay in a whimpering heap at the bottom of a pit. The dragonfly flew off like a helicopter, completely unscathed.

Fern limped to her feet and clawed the pit's walls. The top of the ledge was just out of reach. Her nose felt a tickle, and she started to cry, but she unhinged her claws and wiped her tears when she heard a voice overhead.

"What do we have here?" the familiar voice said. It was pitch-black, but a broad smile lit up the pit. "Aw, are you okay, sweetie?"

Fern sniffled and lowered her guard. Bernadette could calm a worm in a bird's nest. Hack and Shrapnel appeared next to her though, and Fern saw through the hoax.

Shrapnel dug his claws into his neck. "I want an arm and a leg."

Fern barked for help. Hack rolled his eyes. Bernadette kicked Shrapnel into the pit.

"Agh!" Shrapnel said. Debris flew in the air. Fern barked louder.

"Shut her up," Bernadette said.

Shrapnel stretched his arms out wide. Fern backed against the wall and gulped.

*Pffft.* Something whizzed by Hack's head, nicking a neck feather. The tail end of a spear twanged in a tree. Bernadette's smile vanished.

"Hack? Bernie?" Shrapnel said from the bottom of the pit. "What's going on up there?" Fern tilted her head. Shrapnel aimed a claw. "I have to check on something. Don't go anywhere."

Shrapnel pulled himself over the ledge. The first thing he saw was the spear. The next was the world passing him by. He flew headfirst, bounced like a rock kicked off of a tree, and landed on his brother and sister.

Shank lifted Fern like a puppy and held her at eye level. "You rang?" he said. Fern shivered in his grasp. "Sure are an ugly one, aren't you?"

Fern nibbled Shank's finger. His skin sharpened her teeth.

Bernadette elbowed Shrapnel into Hack. Hack shoved Shrapnel back. Shank plucked his spear from the tree. The raptors mummified. Bernadette grinned nervously.

"What should we do with them?" Shank said.

Fern smirked like Betty.

* * *

Delilah used her hands like muffs to cover Ash's ears.

"We're going to find her," Odin said.

"Why weren't you watching her?" said Betty. "Isn't that what you said earlier?"

"Blaming isn't going to help," said Odin. "Calm down. Let's retrace her steps."

"Let's see," Betty said. "She crawled over to you. You fell asleep. And she ran off."

"You don't know that," said Odin. "You weren't paying any attention."

A branch crunched. Odin and Betty unhinged their claws. Delilah looked up and choked.

"You've got to be kidding me," Odin said. He lowered his talons.

Shank stepped forward with Fern on his shoulder. "Is this what you're looking for?"

CHAPTER TWELVE
# THE SLEEPING GIANT

"Fern!" Betty cried. She sprinted and pried Fern from her perch. "You are in so much trouble. And you!" Betty said, glaring at Shank.

"When were you going to tell me I was an uncle?" Shank asked.

Betty smacked Shank across the face. "That's for leaving," she said. She threw her arms around him and hugged him warmly. "This is for coming back."

Odin frowned. Delilah pretended to gag. Odin cleared his throat.

"Where have you been, Shank?"

"Away. I needed time to think."

"About what?" said Odin. "Eating other Carnies?"

Shank squinted. "Why would you say something like that?"

"I don't know," Odin said. "The jungle has ears, you know?"

"Sounds like it has a big, fat mouth on it too," said Shank. Delilah scoffed. Shank gave Odin a fifth of a shrug.

"Okay," said Betty. "I think what Odin meant to say was thank you for cleaning up his mess, and that we're all very happy to have you home."

"Barf," Delilah said under her breath.

"It's good to be back," Shank said. He shifted his shoulders and pretended Delilah was invisible. "But I'm not here to waste any time. I have a plan that could feed all of us for over a month. You're all going to hate it, I promise." Shank turned his head. "Wait, who's missing?"

"Very funny," Delilah said. She uncrossed her arms and put her hands on her hips.

"Not you, dingbat," said Shank. "Where's Michael?"

\* \* \*

Shank's and Odin's tails cut through ferns like scythes.

"Died in the Bad Lands looking for Herbies," Shank said. "There aren't even any plants out there. You can't make this stuff up."

"A little sensitivity would be nice," said Odin. "Betty is still in shambles."

"She'll get over it," said Shank. "And you'll be glad he's not here for this."

"What is 'this' exactly?" Odin asked.

Shank stopped and poked his head through the ferns. An ugly smile transformed his face, and he tugged Odin's arm. Odin parted the ferns and peered over the cliff. Poseidon's neck stuck out like a head on a stick. Odin closed the ferns like drapes.

"Impossible," Odin said. "You're out of your mind."

"Improbable, perhaps," said Shank.

"I thought they migrated," said Odin. "Why isn't he with the rest of them?"

"You mean why would one boneheaded dinosaur abandon his pack?"

Odin fumed. "Salt water on an open wound."

"Don't go all Betty on me," said Shank. "Besides, my plan is flawless."

"Even if it were, we'd need ten more bodies."

"Five by my count," Shank said. "And I know where to get them."

"Oh yeah?" said Odin. "Where?"

Shank grinned widely. "You're not going to like that either."

\* \* \*

Three Troodon boys chased each other in circles. Two were tall and would have been identical if one wasn't covered in spots. The third was a featherless runt. The freckled twin tagged the runt and jaunted away. The runt swiped thrice at his non-spotted brother, whiffing on all three counts. Freckles snuck up behind him and curled into a ball. The standing twin bucked. The runt flinched and tumbled over the freckled twin's back. The bullies snickered and high-fived.

"There you are," a female Troodon said. It was the Troodon mother that had chased Dino Mike through the woods.

The runt sat up like a dust mite covered in brush. A chunk of dirt with an earthworm fell from his head. The twin bullies tensed.

"What the—"

A bush rustled. The Troodon mother hissed and brandished her claws. Odin, armed with a spear, walked out with his hands up. Slowly, he set the spear down and kicked it over. It rolled within an inch of the Troodon's feet. She kicked it back.

"I just want to talk," Odin said. "Where are the others?"

The Troodon mother hissed again. Odin flinched and fell backward into the bush. The bullies howled with laughter. The runt slurped the earthworm like a piece of spaghetti.

* * *

Ash and Fern glared. The Troodon boys glowered back. Their mother, Trina, mutilated Delilah with her stare. Delilah gulped and grinned nervously. Betty sat neutrally between them.

"Where's he at?" Randy, the larger Troodon male, said. He, Odin, and Grego, the shorter Troodon, stood with their arms crossed.

"He's close," Odin said. "I can hear him."

"That's what you said ten minutes ago," said Grego.

"Because I heard him ten minutes ago," said Odin. "Do you even hunt?"

A branch crunched. Eyeballs peppered the woods. Shank escorted three prisoners at spearpoint. Fern hid behind Betty. Ash lowered her brow.

"This is your grand plan?" Odin said. "Raptors?"

"Yes. Raptors," Shank replied. "And Troodons. And deinonychuses. Do you want to go over all the things we don't like about each other, or can we get down to business?"

Awkward silence followed.

"Let's talk turkey," said Shank.

The sun set. Delilah's bony fingers braided vine into rope. At her hip, Fern yawned and snuggled with Ash. Delilah cracked her back slyly and tried to check on her neighbor's progress. Trina had two spools of rope already finished and was starting on a third. She gave Delilah a dirty look.

Shank dunked his hand in a puddle of mud and smeared his face with war paint. He spun around when Betty walked up behind him.

"Your makeup's running," Betty said. "Here." She licked her finger and wiped his cheek. "That's better. Now you look fierce."

Randy, Grego, and Odin whittled long branches into spears. Delilah strolled over with Ash and Fern asleep in her arms. Odin lowered his weapon. "What's up?"

"The rope's done," Delilah said. "Should I start getting ready?"

"You're not coming," Shank said. He walked over and grabbed a spear. "We don't need any distractions."

"I'm not a distraction. I'm a hunter," said Delilah. "Tell him, Odin."

"I can't," Odin said. "He's running this show, and it's a dangerous one. There's no guarantee we'll all make it back."

Delilah's nose tingled. Her eyes welled up. "But—"

"No buts," Odin said. "That's final."

Betty took the girls from Delilah. Fern snorted. Ash smiled in her sleep.

"You are all coming back," Betty said. "With food for all of us."

Odin kissed Ash and Fern on the foreheads. "Daddy has to go to work now," he said. "Behave for your mama."

He leaned in to give Betty a kiss too, but she turned her head, and his peck landed on her cheek.

"We'll see you when you get back," Betty said. "Be safe out there."

\* \* \*

Shank parted a bush and wiped his nose. He was ready for battle. Odin craned his neck and held his breath. They wore spools of rope around their necks, the ends of which were tied to spears.

Poseidon, his face planted on bark, snored and spewed semi-masticated leaves.

"He's a lot bigger up close," Odin said.

Across the way and fit with bandoliers of their own, Bernadette, Hack, and Shrapnel scurried to the base of a tree. Hack and Bernie looked ferocious with their faces painted like Shank's. Shrapnel looked atrocious, like makeup on the backside of a pig.

"Who are you trying to scare?" Hack said. "There are no children here."

Bernadette cleared her throat. Hack and Shrapnel stooped to give her a lift. Bernadette climbed the tree.

"Everyone's in position," Shank said. He ducked back into the bush. "Are you ready?"

"No," Odin said. He drew a breath. "This isn't safe."

"We'll be careful," Shank snarked.

Odin took another breath, this one deeper than the last. "It's desperate. We should go back. It's not a good plan."

Shank gritted his teeth. "It never is if you don't think of it."

Shank shot out of the bush. Reluctantly, Odin ran after him. In silence, they charged Poseidon's hind legs. Randy and Grego attacked from the front. Odin and Shank planted their spears and circled in opposite directions. The ropes unraveled and wrapped around Poseidon's legs. Randy and Grego dipped, and Odin and Shank hopped their spools in passing. At Poseidon's front, Shank pulled his rope taut. Odin ducked to avoid decapitation. Behind Poseidon, the Troodons passed each other with ease.

Bernadette landed with a branch full of meaty leaves. She waved it at Hack and Shrapnel, who were tidying up a trip wire suspended between two distant trees.

Odin and Shank met again at Poseidon's rear. This time, Shank went for Odin's knees. Odin skipped Shank's rope without breaking stride. The Troodons executed another smooth pass up front.

Bernadette reached Poseidon and ran up his tail. She crossed Poseidon's back like it was a tightrope, using her branch as a balancing pole, and tilted her head when she reached his towering neck.

Hack twanged the trip wire with a claw. "It's ready," he said. "Do you see anything?"

Shrapnel made binoculars with his hands and checked in on the action. "Not yet."

With the branch in her mouth, Bernadette pulled herself atop Poseidon's head. Wobbling to keep her balance, she lowered her center of gravity and swung the branch like a flag.

"That's the sign," Shrapnel said. "Let's wake this dude up."

Hack spit in his hand and grabbed a lemon-shaped stone. He hopped like a crow and launched it. The rock fell short by a mile.

"I have to do everything myself," Bernadette said. She bonked Poseidon with the branch on the nose. Poseidon growled, and his bloodshot eyes sprang open. Bernadette dangled the leaves in front of him like a carrot on a string. Poseidon caught a whiff and wagged his tongue.

"He's going to go for it," Shank said. He dug his feet into the ground and pulled the end of his rope with the bulk of his weight. "Hold tight!"

Sure enough, Poseidon's eyes narrowed. He lifted a leg and took a step forward, but the tree branch didn't get any closer. Another step. Same result. Poseidon bit his tongue and built up a head of steam, but the leaves stayed a step ahead of him. Meanwhile, the ropes constricted around his knees.

Bernadette steered Poseidon in the direction of Hack and Shrapnel. The ropes tightened, pulling Poseidon's legs together. With a last-ditch effort, Poseidon hopped like a monopod and sprang for his treat. The Carnies let go of their ropes. Hack and Shrapnel dove out of the way. Poseidon hit the trip wire, toppled over, and crashed to the ground. Bernadette went flying.

A mushroom cloud of dust settled. The Carnies were stunned.

"What are you waiting for?" Shank said. "Attack!" He pulled his spear from the ground and launched it at Poseidon's rump. It stuck, but Poseidon didn't flinch. His only concern was the branch of leaves on the ground in front of him.

"Attack!" Shank repeated.

Odin, Randy, and Grego launched their spears. With three thunks, they sank into Poseidon's hide, causing little in the way of damage.

Poseidon stretched out his tongue and reached for the leaf. A single taste bud latched on like a suction cup, and Poseidon reeled the snack in. The look on his face said it all. In the history of the Good Lands, never had there been a happier dinosaur.

"Our spears aren't working," Odin said. "We have to abort."

Shank ignored Odin and unleashed a bloodthirsty roar. He lunged for Poseidon's neck, slashed his claws with fury, and clamped his jaws with malicious intent. Poseidon's eyes popped out, and a blood vessel bulged in the middle of his forehead. He swung his neck around and bounced Shank's body off the side of a tree. Odin watched in disbelief.

Poseidon stood and flexed his legs. The ropes snapped like rubber bands. Randy and Grego had seen enough. They took off. Odin froze in horror. Poseidon roared and reared on his hind legs. Shank got to his feet in a daze. He had no idea what was above him.

"Shank!" Odin yelled. Shank didn't hear him. Odin bolted and dove. He tackled Shank as Poseidon brought his legs down. Poseidon's hooves landed a foot from Odin's face.

Odin clambered and helped pull Shank up. "Get off me," Shank said. He shoved Odin to the ground.

Poseidon roared and snapped his tail like a whip. Shank jumped and barely cleared it. The tail flew over Odin, who lay facedown. Odin popped up and sent Shank a look like a dagger. Poseidon's tail whipped back around, and Shank gasped. The tail struck Odin in the abdomen and launched him through the air.

Poseidon huffed and puffed. He was ready to bring the whole house down, but a juicy treetop changed his tune. His scowl turned to a smile, and the twinkle returned to his eye. He marched toward the treetop and forgot about the Carnies.

Odin hunched on the ground, unable to breathe. Shank knelt beside him.

"How bad is it?" Odin asked.

Shank couldn't even look. Instead, he helped sit Odin up. "It's not so bad," Shank stuttered. "You're going to be fine."

"Really?" Odin sputtered. "Because it feels like I got cut in half."

"You're not any uglier than you were before," said Shank. "I promise."

"Ha," said Odin, but laughing hurt more than it helped. "You know what the funny thing is? Your stupid plan almost worked."

"Almost," Shank said. "Maybe we can try it again tomorrow."

Odin held his breath. Like raindrops on windowpanes, tears streamed down his face. "Brother, I'm sorry if I've ever done you wrong."

"Shh," Shank said. "You haven't. There's no need to be."

"Yes, there is," said Odin. "I should have listened to you more. But I want you to know everything I ever did was for the good of the pack."

Shank wiped the corner of his eye and whispered in Odin's ear, "Me too. I forgive you."

A sharp pain seared Odin's stomach. Odin tried to look at Shank, but Shank wouldn't meet his stare. Instead, they looked up at the moon together. It formed a perfect crescent.

"Tell Betty I love her," Odin said. "Take care of the girls for me."

Shank laid Odin down and closed his eyelids. Randy, Grego, Bernadette, Hack, and Shrapnel wobbled over. They were battered, beaten, and speechless.

"What did you do?" Bernadette said.

"Nothing," said Shank. He wiped the red tip of his spear off in the dirt. "It was that beast who killed him. Bring his body home and dig him a hole. Make it somewhere nice."

CHAPTER THIRTEEN
# EGGS BENEDICT

A buzzard of a horsefly parked its caboose on a stinking iguanodon's sweat-stained neck. The iguanodon swatted the bug, bursting it and an underlying blister to bits. Contessa clamped her beak and heaped the iguanodon's plate full of olives. The ungrateful iguanodon gagged.

"Next!" Contessa said.

Norm gimped forward. Like the rest of Harvey Plates's gang of ditchdiggers, his body was falling apart, and his hands were covered in boils. Insects orbited like he was a landfill.

"Ew!" Contessa said. "I thought the last one was ripe."

"Quit squawking," said Norm. "Harvey's working us to death." He scowled at the olives. "Is it too much to ask to come home to a decent meal? This slop's not fit for a dung beetle."

"You'd be the expert on dung beetles," said Contessa. She dumped her scoop on Norm's plate. A fly landed, took one whiff, and toppled over. Two out of six legs twitched.

"Next!" Contessa yelled.

Harvey Plates pitched olives into his mouth and ogled Dino Mike across the main table. Granny angled her rocker away and breathed exclusively from the far corner of her mouth.

"What's up with Harvey?" Dino Mike asked. His olives sat untouched in front of him, stacked in a pyramid.

Harmonica looked up and swallowed. "What do you mean?" Beside her, Sonny and Eggbert copied Dino Mike's olive pile.

"He looks like he wants to eat me," said Dino Mike.

"He looks like Harvey to me," said Harmonica.

Groober Spinx pulled out the seat next to Harvey's with a plate of olives in hand. His nostrils flared, and his nose hairs disintegrated. He slid the chair back in.

"Long day at work?" Groober said.

Harvey grunted. Groober shuffled over, grabbed Penny's empty seat, and dragged it as far away as he could without physically leaving the table. When he sat, he knitted his brows at Dino Mike. With an exaggerated motion, he popped an olive into his mouth.

"What's up with Groober?" Harmonica said.

"Huh?" said Dino Mike.

"He looks like he wants to eat you."

Dino Mike shrugged. "He looks like Groober to me." Harmonica slugged him. Dino Mike rubbed his shoulder.

Harvey snuffled and slammed his empty plate on the table. When he was certain nobody was looking, he held up a fist, fake-coughed, and sniffed his underarm. A pungent odor stung his nose.

"Did he just smell his armpit?" Dino Mike said. "Gross."

\* \* \*

A lightning bug exploded over Penny Plates's retina, splattering her eye socket with fluorescent-green goop. Penny dug the sludge out and let her bamboo cable go like a tape measure. The drill bit crashed down.

*Ka-chunk!*

Brute and Taddle lowered a palm tree pipe into the trench. Half of it hung out, spilling into the dry riverbed. Brute lined it up with the pipe behind it. Taddle pushed and locked it in place. They stood in silence. The water tree was a quarter mile away.

Anna stood in the riverbed. A dam of boulders surrounded her like an amphitheater with tightly packed seats. She thrust her arms in the air. "Woo!"

Brute gave Taddle a high five. The slap reverberated for miles.

Penny reeled the bamboo cable in. The drill bit climbed the derrick like a sloth, and Penny's body swayed with every pull. Fatigued, she coiled the loose cable around her wrist, laid her head against the side of the tower, and let her eyes close to catch a wink.

"Penny!" Anna yelled.

Penny jolted. The coil unraveled. The drill bit dropped.

*Ka-chunk!*

Anna flinched. Brute and Taddle buried their faces. Penny bore into Anna with booger-crusted eyes.

"What?" Penny said.

"The, um, pipes are done," Anna said. "How's drilling going?"

Penny opened her mouth. The ground tremored behind her. She closed her mouth and turned. A deep rumbling built to a crescendo. At its peak, the ground went still. Penny looked at Taddle. Taddle looked to Brute. Brute looked at Anna.

Anna shrugged. "What are you looking at me for?"

The well's wormhole belched, blasting the drill bit like a torpedo. It blew the top clean off the derrick, and a torrent of water followed, spewing like oil from the rig.

Overhead, the forgotten drill bit reached the peak of its parabola. It inverted, took a dive, and screamed back to earth.

"Look out!" Penny shouted.

Anna, Brute, and Taddle locked arms with each other. The drill bit lodged in the dirt like a fence post behind them. Penny let out a whoosh of air. Behind her, the well's pressure withered. Penny put her face to the running water and sipped.

"Up top," Anna said, raising a hand. Brute slapped it.

\* \* \*

Groober Spinx stood, arms crossed, under a palm tree at the entrance to the supper grounds. His tail tapped the ground involuntarily.

"Groober, is everything all right?" Harmonica asked. She held Eggbert in her arms. Dino Mike and Sonny walked at her side.

"Peachy," Groober said.

"What's with the ambush?" said Harmonica.

"Nothing serious. Just need a quick chat with Dino Mike."

Mike bit his tongue. He found the thought of pulling an abscessed tooth more appealing.

"Go for it," Harmonica said. "But make it quick. We have to get Sonny and Eggbert home to Granny. It's almost time for bed."

"This'll only take a minute," said Groober. He grabbed Dino Mike's elbow and pulled him down a path. "What are you still doing here?"

"Walking off this supper," Dino Mike said, patting his belly. "Contessa really outdid herself today."

"Don't get cute with me," said Groober. "Why haven't you left?"

"I tried," Dino Mike said. "I must have righted instead. Hard to tell the difference sometimes, wouldn't you agree?"

"You have jokes," Groober said. "That's adorable. I see I'm wasting my time here when I should be talking to Granny."

"Wait," said Mike. "You're right, Groober. I mean, Mr. Spinx. In my two days here, you've treated me better than my family ever has. I would never do anything to put any of you in harm's way, I promise. And I was planning on leaving tonight, I really was. But I'm asking respectfully, begging even, will you please consider letting me stay one more night?"

"For what?"

Dino Mike leaned in. "Harmonica asked me out. She wants to watch the meteor shower with me. I've never been on a date before."

"Well, that's just great," Groober said. "You don't want to eat her. You just want to eat her heart." Groober glanced at Harmonica, who was talking to Miranda under the palm tree. "What is she doing here?"

With droopy eyes, Sonny clung to Harmonica's leg. Harmonica was flustered. "Are you sure it can't wait, Miranda?"

"No," Miranda said. "You have to see for yourself, and you have to see it now. It'll only take a minute, I promise."

"Hey, Miranda," Dino Mike said.

"Dino Mike," said Miranda. She lowered her brow. "Groober."

Groober averted his eyes. "Miranda."

"Is everything all right?" Dino Mike asked.

"I guess not," Harmonica said. She passed Eggbert to Dino Mike. "Miranda has to show me something. Can you watch the kids for a sec?"

Dino Mike's mouth watered. He flexed his abs, trying to muffle his stomach, but it rumbled royally anyway. Groober blinked rapidly.

"You okay?" Harmonica said.

"Totally fine," said Dino Mike. He passed Eggbert back to Harmonica. "Why don't we just go with you? I don't want anybody to get the wrong idea."

"Good point," said Harmonica. "Miranda?"

"That's fine," Miranda said. "Groober can come too. I want him to see this."

Down at the reservoir, Harvey Plates broke the water's surface like a beluga whale and spit water from his blowhole. He whistled, splashed, and scrubbed the filth from his pits.

"This isn't the bathing pool," Miranda said behind a brown bush. She pointed to a ring of mud around a mostly dry puddle. "That was. He's polluting our drinking water."

"Gross," Sonny said loudly. Harvey looked up. Everyone ducked.

"Shh," Harmonica said.

"That's it," Miranda whispered. "We are officially out of water. We don't have a choice anymore. We have to go back to the Good Lands."

"Don't be ridiculous," said Groober. "Just because that's what you've wanted all along, doesn't make it the right thing to do."

"Something told me you'd have an opinion," Miranda said. "Go on. Let's hear it."

"Well, for one, the new water is probably already flowing," Groober said.

"Probably?" said Miranda. "Sounds speculative."

"For another, that water is still waist-deep," said Groober. "Even Harvey isn't dirty enough to pollute volume like that. It should last another two weeks at least, although I do agree we should put some of your restrictions in place."

"I am not drinking Harvey's bathwater," Miranda said. "You can't make me."

"Don't you know how dissolution works?" Groober asked. "How about parts per million? Or basic math, for that matter? Harmonica, please, tell Miranda she's being irrational."

"I can't," Harmonica said. "I think I agree with her."

"You're joking," Groober said.

"I don't know a lot about dissolution," said Harmonica. "But I do know I won't drink stegosaurus broth. And I miss the Good Lands, Groober. So does everyone. If Michael says it's safe to go back, there isn't much left to debate."

Dino Mike tensed under the radiation of Groober's X-ray vision.

"Would you like to weigh in at all, Mr. Deinonychus?" Groober asked.

"I, um, well, um . . ." Dino Mike started. His mouth was dry enough to drink from Harvey's bathtub. "I don't think you should rush into anything."

"What do you mean?" said Harmonica.

"It's just, you have a lot going for you out here, with your garden and everything. And you built it all yourselves," Dino Mike said. "I don't think it's a decision that should be taken lightly, nor should it be one that one or two Herbies get to make. It affects everybody."

Harmonica sighed. "That's a good point," she said. "Why don't we sleep on it, Miranda? We'll gather everyone for a vote tomorrow. I'll take the results to Granny myself. We just can't let Harvey find out."

"Fine," Miranda said. "But I'm casting my ballot now."

Dino Mike held his breath. He knew he couldn't let the secret vote actually take place. He also knew Groober wouldn't, but at least he'd bought them some time.

\* \* \*

Anna and Brute thrust down on a pair of bamboo hoof-straps, driving a lever attached to a hulking wooden pressure pump. A counterweight on the front pulled up and dropped again, forcing a cylindrical piston back down the wormhole. Water poured from a spout, filling the hand-dug reservoir that fed into the pipes.

Anna stuck her tongue out at Brute.

"Stop that," Brute said.

"Stop what?" said Anna, playing it cool.

"You know what."

They kept pumping. Anna stuck her tongue out again.

"Brute, Anna," Taddle said. He ran over, wheezing for breath. "You need to see this."

Anna and Brute stopped pumping. Concern flooded Anna's face. Brute stuck out his tongue. Anna let go of her strap. The lever swung up and pulled out Brute's foot.

"Whoa!" Brute said. He fell on his rump. Anna guffawed.

Penny waited a third of the way down the trench. Behind her, a damp log leaked water. The dry ground drank it all up.

"It's just a small leak," Brute said. "Doesn't look so bad to me."

Penny sank her fist into the log. It crumbled like mulch. She lifted a chunk. It was crawling with termites.

"Gross," Anna said.

"It's infested," said Penny.

"Yeah, but it's just one log, right?" said Anna. "I mean, can't we just replace it?"

Penny kicked the pipe behind her. Termites spilled out like packing peanuts. Anna covered her mouth.

"How many are like that?" Brute asked. Taddle and Penny exchanged looks.

\* \* \*

A wet trail of footprints followed Harvey out of the reservoir. He shook his bald head and patted himself dry with a handful of leaves.

"Psst," someone whispered.

Harvey jumped and peered around. A figure hid in the shadows. "Spinx?" Harvey said. He looked both ways and walked over. "Are you spying on me?"

"Hardly," said Groober. "But others might be. We need to talk."

"About what?"

"About the secret vote Harmonica and Miranda are holding tomorrow. They want to go back to the Good Lands."

"You're lying," Harvey said.

"I'm not," said Groober. "The Carnie is helping them. We need to stop it."

"I'll kill him," Harvey said.

"No," said Groober. "That would backfire and make their case stronger. We have to be smart about this."

"How?"

"By using the Carnie's weakness against him."

"I see," Harvey said. "What's his weakness, again?"

"Eggs," said Groober. "Dino Mike loves eggs."

CHAPTER FOURTEEN
# BOOM GOES THE DYNAMITE

The mouth of Granny Pacquiao's cave grinned like a jack-o'-lantern on the fifth of November. Dancing fireflies flooded the front porch, and an ocean of stars scintillated in the sky. Amid the silence, a spiky shadow slid over a stalagmite.

Ethereal beams of moonlight carved the cave's interior into slices like a cake. The shadowy creature advanced like the lights were rigged to an alarm. One of them grazed the bottom of a face with two sets of tusks. Groober Spinx fidgeted. A spotlight in the corner shone on his objective. Eggbert slept in a nest atop a pedestal.

Groober took a step and clamped a hand over his mouth. A chill rattled his quills. Granny Pacquiao rocked in a chair not ten feet in front of him. Her eye was wide-open.

Groober held his breath, but Granny didn't say a word. She was stiff like a cocoon and breathed so quietly her decibel level might have been negative. Groober squinted. Her eyelid wasn't open after all. The back of it had been painted to look that way.

With a whoosh, Groober let out his breath. Leaves rustled behind him. In a bed beside Eggbert, Sonny rolled over and yawned. His eyes locked onto Groober, and Groober whimpered. Sonny snored like a moose. The back of his eyelids were painted like his grandmother's.

\* \* \*

On one side of her pergola, Harmonica slept like a rock. On the other, Dino Mike's bed was both empty and made. Dino Mike stood at the foot of it, rehearsing all the things he wished he had the luxury to say, "goodbye" and "thank you" being chief among them. He ducked under the awning and accidentally kicked Harmonica's aloe plant over. Harmonica sat up.

"What's going on?" Harmonica said.

"Huh? Nothing," said Dino Mike. He stood the plant up. "What's going on with you?"

Harmonica noticed Dino Mike's bed. "Are you going somewhere?"

"Who? Me? Psh, no."

"Why aren't you sleeping?"

"I, uh, thought I heard something outside. I was going to check it out, and this plant jumped me from out of nowhere. I had to nunchuck it to make sure you were safe."

Harmonica smirked. "Go to bed. You don't want Harvey to catch you outside after dark."

"Right," Dino Mike said. He frowned.

* * *

A raucous ruckus ripped Harmonica from her sleep. Dino Mike rolled out of bed and covered his neck, suspecting an earthquake. Harmonica knew better, however. Somebody, or something, was coming down her staircase.

Outside, Harvey, Norm, and their gang of iguanodon goons had the pergola surrounded. "We know you're in there, Carnie," Harvey said. "Come out with your hands up."

Dino Mike exchanged looks with Harmonica. "Wait here," Harmonica whispered. She stepped outside.

"Harmonica," Harvey said. "Top of the morning to you."

"Oh, shove it," said Harmonica. "What do you want?"

"There's been an eggnapping," Harvey said. "We're here to investigate."

"That's ridiculous," said Harmonica.

"Be that as it may, if you don't step aside, I'll have you restrained."

"You wouldn't dare."

Harvey tilted his head. Norm and another iguanodon hooked Harmonica's arms. Harvey waved his hand. The other two iguanodons entered the shelter and dragged Dino Mike out.

"Let go of him!" Harmonica yelled. "And let go of me!" She struggled and stomped Norm's foot, but she was unable to break free.

"Agh!" Norm said. "Hold still."

Harvey got up in Dino Mike's grill. "Do you have something to say for yourself?"

"I didn't do anything," Dino Mike said.

"We'll see about that," said Harvey. He dipped under the canopy, tilted the aloe plant over, and stooped to pick something up. He turned and held Eggbert up for everyone to see. Harmonica stopped fighting. Harvey passed her the egg.

"That wasn't me," Dino Mike said. "They planted him there, Harmonica. I'm innocent, I swear."

"Save it for the jury," Harvey said. He nodded to the others. "Take him upstairs. Norm?"

"Yeah, Harvey?"

"Bring me Corrine."

The iguanodons marched Dino Mike up to the supper grounds. Most of the other Herbies were already there, mumbling like radio static. Groober stood conspicuously, front and center. Dino Mike looked to him for assistance. Groober stared at the dirt.

"That's good," Harvey said, pointing to the empty space in front of the main table. The iguanodons forced Dino Mike to his knees, and Dino Mike bit his tongue. "Where's Norm?" said Harvey.

"Here," Norm said, dragging the battle-axe behind him. It carved a channel in the dirt. "This thing is heavy."

Harvey lifted the axe without effort and loomed over Dino Mike. "No sense beating around the bush here. In the matter of the Carnie versus the Great Lands, I find you guilty of eggnapping and sentence you to die. Do you have any last words?"

"You mentioned a jury?" Dino Mike said.

"I am the jury," said Harvey.

"I've been framed," Dino Mike said. Harmonica coddled Eggbert with teary eyes. "I had nothing to do with this, Harmonica. I don't care what happens to me. I just want you to know that."

"Duly noted," Harvey said. "If there are no further objections, we can proceed."

Harmonica shielded Eggbert and turned away. Harvey wiped his nose. The iguanodons pressed down on Dino Mike's shoulders, exposing his neck.

"Harvey!" a voice yelled. The gathered Herbies turned their heads.

"What is it?" Harvey said. "Who's there?"

Brute Grimstone shoved his way through the Herbies and stooped with a stitch in his side. "Harvey," he gasped. "We need to talk."

"I'm a little busy at the moment."

Brute looked around. "I'm not sure what's going on here, but what I have to say is important."

"I'll be with you in a moment," said Harvey.

"It can't wait," said Brute.

"It'll have to," said Harvey. He spit in his palms and gripped the axe handle. Brute pieced things together and sobered up. Harvey lifted the axe. Dino Mike smiled sadly.

"Put that thing down," another voice said. This one was cold and shrill. Harvey winced. *Click. Tick. Tack.* Granny Pacquiao advanced. Sonny held her hand.

"Grandmother," Harvey said. "You're right on time. I was about to administer justice."

"I said drop it," Granny repeated. "Let the Carnie go. He didn't do it."

"With all due respect, Grandmother, I have physical evidence to suggest otherwise."

"Your evidence is bogus," Granny said. "It couldn't have been him."

"Why not?" said Harvey.

"Because he doesn't have quills," said Granny. She held one up.

The Herbies gasped and murmured. Groober tucked his head in an imaginary shell. Dino Mike glared. Harvey Plates lowered his weapon.

"Groober, how could you?" Harmonica asked.

"I didn't have a choice," Groober said. "I couldn't let your secret vote happen."

"What vote?" Granny demanded.

"The vote to return to the Good Lands," Groober said.

"But why?" said Harmonica.

"It isn't safe," said Groober. "This Carnie might not eat other dinosaurs, but the other Carnies still do. A pack of raptors tried to eat me the last time I was there."

"Is that true?" Harmonica said.

"It is," Dino Mike admitted.

"Then why did you come here?" said Harmonica.

Dino Mike took a deep breath. "My family was starving to death," he said. "They *are* starving to death. I thought if I could find you all, then maybe I could trick you into coming back so they could eat. But I changed my mind when I met you."

The crowd froze. Harmonica stepped forward. Dino Mike's puppy dog eyes begged her forgiveness. Harmonica slapped his face.

"I was wrong about you," she said.

Miranda wriggled through elbows and knees and forced her way to the frontline. "This doesn't change anything, Harmonica," Miranda said. "We're still out of water. Carnies or no Carnies, if we don't go back to the Good Lands, we'll all die of thirst."

"We've been over this a thousand times," Harvey said. "The water is on the way."

Brute cleared his throat. "Yeah, about that."

"What?" said Harvey. "What is it?"

"The drill and the pump both work perfectly, just like Groober said they would. But—"

"But what?"

"Some of the pipes are leaking. They're overrun with termites."

"How many is some?" Harvey asked.

"Anywhere from most to all," said Brute.

"It's settled then," Miranda said. "Grandmother?"

"One thing at a time," Granny said. "We can debate this later. Right now, we have a lying Carnie to kill."

"What? No!" Sonny yelled.

"Yes!" said Harvey. A disgusting smile warped his face. The iguanodons pressed down on Dino Mike's back.

"Must we do this, Grandmother?" Harmonica said. "Is there no other way?"

"The only reason I kept him alive was because I thought he was telling the truth," Granny said. "He fooled me. Now, if he opens his mouth, I don't know what to believe."

"You can't," Sonny said. "He's my friend."

"Pipe down, Sonny," Granny said. She waved at Harvey. "Do it."

"With pleasure," Harvey said.

Harvey swung back the axe. Sonny spotted a rock on the ground. He let go of Granny's hand, ran at full speed, and kicked it. The rock pelted Harvey in the neck, and the axe fell behind him. Sonny lowered his head and rammed one of Dino Mike's captors, buckling his knee. Dino Mike broke free from the other.

"Run, Dino Mike!" Sonny shouted. "Run!"

Dino Mike took off before anyone else could grab him. He skidded by the palm tree at the fork in the path and disappeared around the corner.

"After him!" Harvey shouted.

Dino Mike reached the cul-de-sac of teepees and looked both ways, but he didn't know where to go. He glanced over his shoulder. A horde of Herbies was forming a stampede. An arm looped around his waist and pulled him behind a tent. The angry mob bustled past.

Contessa Treehorn uncovered Dino Mike's mouth and peeked around the corner.

"C'mon," Contessa whispered. "This way."

Contessa led Dino Mike through the olive grove and up to the garden. They trod through the fertilizer to the field of future ferns.

"Run until you reach the riverbed," Contessa said. "You can follow that to the water tree. You're on your own from there."

"Thank you, Contessa," Dino Mike said. "But why are you helping me?"

"Because you were sweet with Sonny and Harmonica," said Contessa. "And you're the only one who doesn't complain about my cooking."

"I have to be honest with you," Dino Mike said. "I didn't really like your olives."

"I know," said Contessa. "But no matter what anyone says, it is okay to lie sometimes." She smiled and gave Dino Mike a small leather satchel. "Here."

"What is it?" He lifted the flap.

"A snack for the road," Contessa said. "In case you get hungry. Now go. Hurry, before they catch up."

Dino Mike gave Contessa a bear hug. "I can't thank you enough," he said. He let go, took a few steps, and stopped.

"What is it?' Contessa said.

"Can you tell Harmonica something for me?"

"No. I can't."

Dino Mike was perplexed. "What? Why not?"

"There is no more Harmonica for you," Contessa said. "Forget about her and forget about here. If you care about her, you will. Now, for the love of all things Herbie, go. Leave. Please. Leave, and don't you ever come back."

## CHAPTER FIFTEEN
# CAMPFIRE SONGS

Dino Mike crossed his eyes. A tiny droplet of water dangled from the edge of the pressure pump's spout, daring gravity to do its dirty work. Dino Mike bit his tongue and traced the pump's counterweight to the lever on the back. He stepped into a hoof-strap. The mechanism nodded like a donkey, and a thin ribbon of water trickled out.

Dino Mike pursed his lips and leaned in. Ice-cold divinity rolled over his tongue. When he swallowed, the water coated his stomach like milk. Dino Mike belched, fell on his bottom, and picked up a stick. The Poseidon constellation shimmered between the cottonwood's balding branches. Dino Mike scribbled a map in the dirt.

Footsteps pattered in the distance. Dino Mike snapped his head around to look. Overhead, a cosmic pebble fizzled in the atmosphere. It was the shower's first meteor.

"I want an exact count," Harvey Plates said. Anna, Taddle, Penny, and Groober followed along the trench.

"Brute's already getting one," said Anna.

"Why aren't you helping?" said Harvey.

"I trust his math," Anna said. "So long as he don't run out of toes."

Harvey stopped walking. Anna, Taddle, and Penny hit the brakes too. Groober crashed into the back of their legs. One of his quills broke off under Taddle Bill's skin.

"Hibiscus!" Taddle shouted. "Dang-dung it, Spinx!"

Groober didn't apologize. With Taddle out of the way, he saw why Harvey had stopped. The lever on the pump rocked ever so slightly, and a hairline of water trickled from the spout.

"Find him," Harvey said.

Penny and Taddle broke off in opposite directions. Groober pulled on a hoof-strap, halting the lever's progress. Anna crossed her arms.

"What are you doing?" Harvey said.

"Nothing," said Anna. "And you can't make me."

"We don't have time for this," said Harvey.

"I don't have time for you," said Anna. "What you did back there wasn't cool."

"You mean what Spinx did?"

"I mean what you both did," said Anna. "This is your pile of dung. You deal with it." She uncrossed her arms and recrossed them for emphasis.

Groober ran his hand along the pump and knelt by the spout. He picked up a stick and noticed Dino Mike's map.

"Agh!" Groober said. He spun around and blocked the map from view.

"What is it?" said Harvey. He pointed to the stick. "And what is that?"

"It's a stick," Groober said. He chuckled and chucked it aside. "It's only a stick." Harvey looked suspicious. "Look," Groober said, pointing. "Brute's back."

Brute climbed out of the trench and dusted off his knees. Groober kicked dirt over Dino Mike's map. Anna raised her eyebrows.

"What's the damage?" Harvey said.

"It's worse than we thought, Harv."

"I want a number. Don't kale-coat it."

"Half of the pipes are completely destroyed," Brute said. "Irreparable."

"The other half?"

"Only partially."

"Drat," Harvey said. "We need to replace the whole dang-dung thing."

"Harvey," Penny said. Harvey looked up. Penny and Taddle had returned. Taddle was out of breath. "There's no sign of him," Penny continued. "We looked everywhere."

"Forget about the Carnie," said Harvey. "Spinx, how much water do we really have left?"

"In a week, it won't be water; it'll be mud," Groober said.

"Could we double that if we had to?" Harvey asked. "If we put McBeek's emergency countermeasures in place?"

"Maybe," said Groober. "But that wouldn't matter unless you had a quarter mile of extra pipe lying around."

"What if I did?"

"Still wouldn't matter. Unless we cleared out all the old logs and eradicated every last termite. Otherwise the new ones would suffer a similar fate. Hypothetically speaking."

"Got it," Harvey said. "Penny, Van Kirk, stay here and help Spinx clear out these logs. If the Carnie comes back, kill it. Grimstone, Bill, you're with me."

"Wait, what?" Groober said. "Where are you going?"

"To tear down a wall," said Harvey. "We have half the pipes already. We can chop down the rest."

"What about the termites?" said Groober.

"Sounds like a Spinx problem to me," Harvey said. "You've got a week. Figure it out."

* * *

Harmonica sat on the boulder in the garden and clutched her knees to her chest. With wet eyes, she took in a symphony of embers raining from space. A column of worker ants marched up the empty seat beside her.

Someone poked Harmonica's shoulder. She turned, and Sonny tackled her like a linebacker. Harmonica squeezed him, and a heavy hand fell on her shoulder. Harmonica looked up. Contessa smiled. Harmonica squeezed Contessa's hand and smiled back.

* * *

An angry pink fireball loomed on the horizon. Heat rose like fumes from the rocky desert surface. Dino Mike's silhouette hobbled along like a bobblehead in the distance. In lapses, he grew larger, and the sun climbed a ladder in the sky.

Full-size and weary, Dino Mike squinted. Either he was seeing a mirage, or the haunted boneyard was just ahead.

Dino Mike's dirty feet glided along a sauropod's tail, stopping outside the giant rib cage with the palm leaf-thatched walls. His shins wobbled, and his weak body swayed. Dino Mike crumpled.

Orange light flickered and danced inside the rib cage. Dino Mike curled under a blanket and took note of the darkness outside. When he remembered he didn't have a blanket, he hopped up like he'd seen a mouse.

"Ew," Dino Mike said. He jabbed the blanket with his foot to make sure it wasn't living. It was not, but it was made of fur, some of which had been singed. It was Groober's poncho. "Double ew."

A delicious aroma hooked Mike by the nostrils and dragged him against his will. An eerie, woodwind melody rode the wind outside. Dino Mike's blood turned cold. He latched onto a protruding rib, but the mighty scent proved irresistible. It pried his digits one by one.

Outside, the music grew louder. It was melancholic but beautiful, the perfect complement to the campfire crackling in the stone pit. The smell also came from the fire. Dino Mike held a wrist to his forehead. A furry, charbroiled tarantula roasted on a spit. It was at least as large as he was. The music cut off.

"Oh good. You're up," a gentle voice said.

Dino Mike turned. A serpent-headed beast with scissors for hands lowered a flute and limped toward him. Each of its blades was over a meter long. Dino Mike ran. The protruding rib clotheslined him, knocking him cold and flat.

While the campfire warmed the smile on Dino Mike's face, the smell of rotisserie arachnid overloaded his olfactory receptors. Mike opened his eyes and sat up. The Therizinosaurus, the demon destined to haunt his dreams forever, snipped a limb from the spider's cephalothorax and latched onto it like a snake.

"Agh!" Dino Mike said, hopping to his feet. The furry blanket fluttered to the ground.

"If you're going to run, watch out for the third rib on the right," the Therizinosaurus said. "It's a real doozy."

Dino Mike put his hands on his hips and scoffed. "Is that supposed to be funny?"

"I don't know," said the Therizinosaurus. "Is your haircut?"

Dino Mike scoffed again.

"Relax," the Therizinosaurus said. "I'm kidding. The name's Gazpacho. You hungry?"

"Gazpacho?" Dino Mike said.

"Sí. Gazpacho." He waved a hand full of scythes. "I'd offer to shake your hand, but—"

"No, I get it," Dino Mike said. He glanced down at the blanket. "Did you tuck me in?"

"What?" said Gazpacho. "No. You were shivering. I was just returning your fur."

"It's not mine."

"Your friend's, then. The pointed one. What was his name?"

"We are not friends," Dino Mike said. "Not anymore."

"That's too bad," said Gazpacho. He snipped another leg from the tarantula and offered it to Mike. "What's yours?"

Dino Mike balked at Gazpacho's hedge clippers. "Are you trying to fatten me up so you can put me on one of those sticks?"

"Would it stop you from eating this delicious spider if I was?"

Gazpacho's logic was sound. Dino Mike took the leg. "Thanks. I'm Dino Mike."

"Dino Mike?" said Gazpacho.

"Sí. Dino Mike."

The tarantula's scent made Dino Mike's mouth water. His stomach churned.

"Let me know how it is," said Gazpacho.

Dino Mike sank his teeth in. Smoky, savory juice seeped out, coating his mouth with umami. He swallowed, and the sensation slid down to his tummy, wrapping his insides in a warm hug.

"Wow. This is the single best thing I have ever eaten," Dino Mike said.

"It's the fire," said Gazpacho. "Everything I've tried so far tastes better cooked."

"Where did you learn how to do that?"

"From you and the pincushion the last time you were here."

"That's right. I saw you," Dino Mike said. "You wrapped your . . . things around the rib cage and scared us with your creepy music."

"That's subjective and hurtful," Gazpacho said. "I make music, period."

"I'm sorry. I didn't mean—"

"No, I get it," said Gazpacho. "I'm hideous. I'm the stuff nightmares are made from."

"That's not true."

"It's not? What was it you did the first time you saw me? And the second?"

Dino Mike removed his foot from his mouth. It left a bitter aftertaste. "So what kind of music do you play?"

"Blues mostly," said Gazpacho. "Little aerobone. Little xylobone. I make my own instruments. Got a lot of material to work with."

"That's fantastic," Dino Mike said. "I dance a little. Nothing too serious. How about you? Dance at all?"

"Not really," said Gazpacho. "Definitely not since I picked up this limp."

Dino Mike glanced down. It was hard to make out from the scabs and bloodstained feathers, but Gazpacho's leg showed evidence of scarring and, perhaps, significant injury.

"Oh no. What happened?" Dino Mike said.

"You don't remember?" said Gazpacho. "How's your head, by the way?"

Dino Mike grabbed his noggin, and it clicked. "The allosaurus? That was you?"

"Yeah. Sorry about the lump, kid. It was for your own protection, I swear."

"But why did you help us?"

"For the same reason you were helping Hokeypokey," said Gazpacho. "It was the right thing to do."

"Your leg might be infected," Dino Mike said. "You should really get that checked out."

"Not a lot of good doctors on my side of town. Not a lot of lands that'll take me."

"I know a girl," Dino Mike said. "I'm not allowed to talk to her though, and if the other Herbies see me anywhere near her, they'll kill me on sight. But she could definitely help."

"Thanks for the tip," Gazpacho said.

"Anytime," said Dino Mike.

There was a brief, awkward silence. Gazpacho broke it.

"What's with the bag?"

"Huh? This?" Dino Mike held up Contessa's satchel. "A triceratops gave it to me. Some sort of bladder, I'm guessing. Those Herbies are resourceful."

"Cute story. What's in it?"

"A snack," Dino Mike said. He dumped the satchel in his hand.

"Olives?" said Gazpacho. "But I thought you were a Carnie?"

"I am," said Dino Mike. "It's a long story."

"You in a hurry?" said Gazpacho.

Dino Mike sighed. "Okay, well, it all started when I met Groober Spinx in the Good Lands, I guess."

"Prickles?"

"Yeah, Prickles. He was about to get eaten by a pack of raptors, and I saved him because, like you said, it was the right thing to do. The thing was, he shouldn't have been there in the first place because none of the other Herbies were. They had disappeared. Turns out he was collecting seeds and samples for a secret garden the Herbies have been growing in a hidden desert oasis."

"Go on."

"Anywho, after I saved him, he dropped a map that led to the oasis. My family has been, and still is, starving because there aren't any Herbies left to eat, so I thought I might use the map to find the Herbies so I could trick them into coming back with me."

"And it backfired?" Gazpacho said.

"How'd you guess?" said Dino Mike. "To make a long story medium in size, the Herbies made me eat olives in front of a jury. For some reason, I was able to hold them down, so they let me stay. Then they found out I was lying, and the triceratops, who was really nice, helped me escape with my life. She gave me the olives for the road in case I got hungry."

"Why don't you feed your family those?"

"The olives?" Dino Mike said. "I'd rather starve, they're so nasty. I have no idea how I didn't puke them up to be honest. I just took the bag to be nice."

"Do you mind if I try?" Gazpacho asked.

Dino Mike tossed the satchel. "Knock yourself out."

"Now where have I seen somebody do that recently?" Gazpacho said. He poked a scissor in the bag, skewered an olive, bit down, and swished the olive around inside his mouth. His face contorted. "Oh, yeah. That's rancid. Like warm booger with a hint of dung."

"Told you," Dino Mike said.

Gazpacho dumped the bag out and skewered the rest of the fruit.

"What are you doing?" Dino Mike asked.

"I told you," Gazpacho said. "Everything I've tried so far tastes better cooked." He roasted the olives like marshmallows over the fire. One went up in flames. Gazpacho blew and flung his hand. The olive flew past Dino Mike's head.

"Whoa. My bad," Gazpacho said. "That one's yours."

"I'm good," said Dino Mike. "Seriously. Thanks."

"Suit yourself," said Gazpacho. He blew on another olive and bit down with closed eyes. He clenched a fist in front of his mouth to savor the lusciousness.

"You're being dramatic," Dino Mike said.

Gazpacho shook his head. He didn't remove his fist or open his eyes. Dino Mike picked up the olive that had flown astray and blew it off. He gave it a whiff and popped it in his mouth. It burned his tongue. Dino Mike panted and bit down. It was warm, juicy, and exquisite, the second-best thing he'd ever eaten.

"Incredible," Dino Mike said. He licked his fingers and teeth and picked up the satchel. "I'm going to need those back."

Gazpacho frowned. "Dino Mike giveth, and Dino Mike taketh away."

"I'm sorry," Dino Mike said. "But I think you just saved my family."

"I see," Gazpacho said. He slid the olives off of his scythes, and his serpent head drooped. "You're leaving, then?"

"I have to," Dino Mike said. "Why don't you come with me?"

"I'm flattered," said Gazpacho. "But with my leg, I would never make it."

Dino Mike winced. He'd forgotten about Gazpacho's leg, something he felt personally responsible for, and shuddered to think what would happen if Gazpacho didn't receive treatment. On the other hand, or in it rather, he had the solution to all of the Carnies' problems. All he had to do was deliver it.

"I have to get these olives to the Good Lands," Dino Mike said. "But after that, I'm coming back, and I'm going to get you the help that you need."

"Why would you do that?" Gazpacho said.

"It's the right thing to do," said Dino Mike. He wrapped the satchel around his wrist, looked up, and found Poseidon in the sky. "I'll be back in a couple of days. Take it easy if you can."

"I'll leave the light on for ya," Gazpacho said.

CHAPTER SIXTEEN
# THE UGLY LANDS

A kaleidoscope of spotted butterflies swarmed the air. An army of furry, green caterpillars mobbed a deciduous tree. Dino Mike planted a big, fat kiss in the Good Lands' soil. He rose and wiped his mouth, and his eyes guzzled the colorful flowers swaying in the breeze.

A treetop under duress snapped back into place. Beneath it, the real Poseidon noshed on some leaves.

"Howdy, stranger!" Dino Mike yelled.

Poseidon glanced down. Dino Mike waved. Poseidon swung his neck like a nine iron and roared in Dino Mike's face.

Dino Mike wiped vegetal sludge from his cheeks. "Good to see you too, buddy."

"Dino Mike," said Poseidon. "I didn't know that was you, my dude. You're not dead?"

"I don't believe it," Dino Mike said. "You remembered more than one name. Who'd you think I was?"

"Hard telling from up there," said Poseidon.

"Why the hostility?"

"You've been gone awhile. The neighborhood ain't what it used to be. I got hunted the other day."

"No. By who?"

"Like I said, it's hard to say," said Poseidon. "I might have actually stepped on one. Or whacked him good with my tail at least."

"Gross."

"Yeah. How'd it go? Find what you were looking for?"

"Actually, yes," Dino Mike said. He clutched his satchel. "I'm taking it to my family right now."

"Awesome," said Poseidon. A scrumptious treetop beckoned, and he grew antsy. "Glad you're back, dude. Let's hang soon."

"Hang?"

"Yeah," said Poseidon. "Like, hang out, you know?" He was already five steps away.

\* \* \*

Giant ferns swayed in their giant field. Dino Mike emerged from the thicket, overflowing with gratitude, and swung his arms as he strolled. The ground collapsed beneath him. Dino Mike smashed his jaw on a ledge and went to sleep.

Nondescript voices muttered. Eyelids opened and closed, revealing blurry splotches of light.

*"How long do you think he's been there?"*

*"Hard to say."*

*"What should we do?"*

*"I don't know. I'm thinking."*

*"What do you think is in the bag?"*

*"Jump down there and find out."*

Dino Mike lay on his back, and his swirling senses converged. Three shadows peered down from a ring at the top of a pit. All three of them had spears.

"He's awake."

Dino Mike sat up. Bernadette, Hack, and Shrapnel scooted back. The pit was three feet deep. Bernadette grinned.

"You?" Dino Mike said. "What is this? What are you doing here?"

"What are you doing here?" Shrapnel said. "Shank said you were dead."

Dino Mike furrowed his brow. Bernadette and Hack smacked Shrapnel's head.

Bernadette nodded. "What'cha got in the bag, mister?"

"Mister?"

"Wasn't that your name? Mr. Mike or something?"

"Dino Mike, actually. But now that you mention it, it's Mr. Deinonychus to you."

"What's in the bag, Mr. Deinonychus?" Bernadette repeated.

"None of your business," said Dino Mike.

"Our hole," Hack said. "That makes it our business."

"Yeah right," said Dino Mike. He stood, and the raptors aimed their spears. Dino Mike held out his palms. "Whoa, whoa, whoa. Why so serious?"

"The bag," said Hack. "Hand it over."

"I can't," Dino Mike said.

"Why not?" said Bernie.

"It's a gift for Odin," said Dino Mike. "I don't know if you know who that is, but he's not someone you want to upset."

The raptors lowered their spears and averted their eyes.

"What?" Dino Mike said.

\* \* \*

Whitecaps rolled and crashed in a vast, blue ocean. The low tide washed up over a seashell-speckled beach.

A round, snooty fish lay dormant in the shallow water offshore. The sun glared, and a spear struck like lightning. It came down an inch too far to the left, however. The muck settled, and the fish flipped up its nose and flitted away.

"I don't get it," Randy said. He and Grego waded knee-deep in the sea. "It's almost like the water bends the light or something."

"Right," said Grego. He stabbed the ocean with a spear of his own. "I'm sure it has nothing to do with your aim."

Fern and the Troodons played tug-of-war on the beach. It was her and the runt versus the twin and Freckles. The runt wasn't very effective, but Fern had the bullies on the ropes. Freckles gritted his teeth. Fern winked. Freckles snarled and kicked up sand. Fern sidestepped and let go of the rope. Freckles and the twin tumbled backward. Fern caught the runt and dusted off her hands.

Delilah, Ash, and Trina lay in the sand, soaking up rays. The tide rinsed off their toes. Delilah fanned herself and watched Randy and Grego fish.

"How long have you and Randy been together?" Delilah asked.

"That's none of your concern," said Trina.

"I'm just trying to start a conversation."

"Do me a favor. Don't."

Grego pulled a puny fish out of the water and waved his spear in celebration. Delilah raised an eyebrow. Randy buried his head.

"What about Grego?" Delilah said.

Betty sat on a log and stared out at the water. She played with a claw, one of Odin's, which dangled like a pendant around her neck. Shank, standing nearby, wore Odin's other claw around his.

"Excuse me," Shrapnel said. "Um, Mr. Shank?"

"Is this important?" Shank said.

"I think so," said Shrapnel.

"Is there a problem? Or did you accidentally catch something in one of your traps?"

Shrapnel was confused. "Both. I think."

Shank tilted his head. Bernadette and Hack guided Dino Mike forward.

"Michael?" Betty said. She stood and threw her arms around him, sobbing relentlessly. "You're home. I knew you'd come home."

"Agh." Dino Mike pushed Betty back and pulled the tip of Odin's claw out of his chest. "What's this? You two got matching jewelry?"

"It isn't like that," Betty said. She choked up. "Odin had an accident. Shank's been doing his best to help keep us together and fed."

"I heard," said Dino Mike. He glared at Shank. "I also heard it might not have been an accident."

"Michael," Betty said. The raptors straightened their spines.

"It's okay," said Shank. He smiled and rested his claws on Dino Mike's shoulders. "You've been gone awhile, and a lot of things have changed. But we're glad to have you home."

Betty sniffled and mopped the bags under her eyes. "What happened out there?" she asked. "Did you find the Herbies?"

"Yeah," Dino Mike said. "I found them. They're dead. All of them."

"What?" said Betty.

"There's a mass graveyard a couple of nights north of here," said Dino Mike. "That's as far as they made it."

"That's too bad," said Shank. He flipped over Dino Mike's wrist. "What's this?"

"The solution to all our problems," Dino Mike said. He unraveled the satchel and handed it over. Shank peeked inside.

"Olives?"

"They're edible," said Dino Mike. "I ate them to survive."

"You ate olives?" said Betty.

"I did," said Dino Mike. "They're bitter when they're raw, but they're delicious when you put a flame to them. Either way, they don't make you sick."

"We're not putting a flame to anything," Shank said.

"You don't have to," said Dino Mike. "They're already cooked. Go on, try one. I bet you change your mind."

Shank looked at Betty like insanity ran in her family. Betty nodded at the satchel. Shank took a whiff. His tear ducts fizzled.

"No way," Shank said. "That's worse than dung. Get it away from me."

"What?" Dino Mike said. He smelled the bag and jerked his nose away. "Oh, gross. What happened?" He dumped the satchel out. The olives were mushy and covered in mold. No wonder they reeked. "They must go bad if you don't eat them right away," Dino Mike continued. "That's okay. I know a grove nearby. We can get more."

"That won't be necessary," Shank said.

"We have to," said Dino Mike. "What will we eat?"

"Anything else," said Shank.

"But—"

"What's he doing here?" an angry voice said.

Dino Mike spun. Randy and Grego had three pathetic fish skewered between them.

"He lives here," Shank said. "Why? Do you know each other?"

Randy and Grego narrowed their eyes. The fish flopped on their sticks.

\* \* \*

A single boulder rested in the shade of a coconut tree. A perfect ocean view went on without bound. Dino Mike bowed his head.

"What's a matter? You don't like fish fins?" a voice said. Dino Mike looked up. Delilah walked over to join him.

"I wasn't hungry," said Dino Mike.

"Yeah, me neither," Delilah said. "Poor Odin. What a shame."

"Yeah."

"It'll be an even bigger shame if he gets away with it," Delilah added.

"What are you talking about?" Dino Mike asked.

"C'mon. You don't really think he fell and landed on his own spear, do you? Word is it was Shank's fault he got whipped in the first place."

"So the raptors were telling the truth? But why?"

"I don't know. It doesn't look like he minds being in charge, though."

Dino Mike peered down the beach. Betty and the girls were building a sand volcano. Shank held discussions with Randy and Grego beyond them.

"What about you?" Delilah asked. "Why did you lie?"

"Come again?' said Dino Mike.

"You said you found all the Herbies dead two days north of here."

"So?"

"What did you do the rest of the time?"

"I, uh, got caught in a storm," Dino Mike said.

"That lasted a week?" said Delilah.

"It was a big storm," said Dino Mike. He dug a seashell out of the sand. Delilah lifted his chin. Dino Mike's heart banged out of his chest.

"It's okay," Delilah said. "I won't tell anyone. You can trust me."

Dino Mike swallowed the lump in his throat.

\* \* \*

Under a sky full of stars, Dino Mike woke up with a hand over his mouth. Shank was so close Mike could taste his sour breath, but it wasn't Shank restraining him. Both of Shank's hands were free.

"Shh, shh, shh, shh," Shank said. "Relax. I just want to talk."

Randy uncovered Dino Mike's mouth, but he didn't let him go.

"What do you want?" Dino Mike asked.

"I want you to take us to the Great Lands," said Shank.

Dino Mike gritted his teeth. "So she did tell you?"

"Who? Delilah?" said Shank. "Of course she did. She tells me everything."

"Then she must have told you that's never going to happen," said Dino Mike. "I don't care what you do to me."

"Yeah, she mentioned that too," Shank said. His grin was incendiary. "Don't worry. I'm not going to touch you. That ugly, little shrimp that looks like you though? I'm going to hurt her really bad."

"You wouldn't," Dino Mike said. He scanned the beach, but he couldn't find Fern. "Betty would never forgive you."

"I'll make it look like an accident," Shank said. "Accidents have been happening a lot around here. Or haven't you heard?"

Dino Mike lunged. Randy clamped his elbow around Dino Mike's throat.

"This isn't up for negotiation," Shank said.

"All right, you win," Dino Mike sputtered. "I'll do whatever you want. Please, don't hurt her." Shank nodded. Randy loosened his choke hold. Dino Mike gasped and grabbed his neck. "We can leave tomorrow night," Dino Mike added.

"So you can have a day to talk your way out of it and warn the others?" Shank said. "I don't think so." His toxic smile widened. "We leave now."

## CHAPTER SEVENTEEN
# GHOST STORIES

*Clack-clack. Clack-clack. Clack-clack.*

The Carnies marched through the desert like a band of mercenaries with spears. The raptors brought up the rear. Shrapnel banged two coconuts together incessantly. Hack peeled his bloodshot eyes. Bernadette pressed her tongue against the back of her teeth to calm her aching nerves.

*Clack-clack. Clack-clack. Clack-clack.*

The Bad Lands were dark and frigid. Randy breathed into cupped hands. Trina wrapped her kids in her arms like burritos. Grego hugged his own shoulders for warmth. Ahead of them, Ash buried her head in Betty's armpit. Fern clung to the nook on Shank Nightcuss's neck. Dino Mike's simmering blood reached a boil.

"Can you believe him?" Delilah said. "I mean, could he be any more obvious?"

Dino Mike didn't dignify her with a response. Instead, he kept his focus skyward and walked the way of Poseidon.

"I'm talking to you," Delilah said. "Are your ears broken?"

"I can hear fine," Dino Mike said. "I just don't have anything nice to say."

"Why?" said Delilah. "Because I told Shank about the Herbies? What did you expect me to do?"

"Anything but that," said Dino Mike. "I trusted you."

"Well, we can't live off fish eyes forever," said Delilah. She glanced over her shoulder and checked on Shank and Betty. "Ugh. If Odin knew how close he was to her, he'd turn over in his grave."

Dino Mike stopped walking. "Are you really that ugly on the inside?"

Delilah's lips quivered.

"What's the holdup?" Shank asked. Fern shrugged on Shank's shoulder, echoing his sentiment.

"There isn't one," Dino Mike said. He marched past Delilah.

*Clack-clack. Clack-clack. Clack-clack.*

Inevitably, the sunrise teased the skyline with wild magenta hues. The mushroom-shaped rocks stood like totem poles, and the Carnies gathered beneath them.

"This is it," Dino Mike said. "We'll camp here for the day."

"The sun's not up," Shank said. "We can go farther."

"Not unless you want to turn into prunes," said Dino Mike. "There isn't any shelter from here to the haunted boneyard."

"Haunted?" Grego said. "What's it haunted by?"

Dino Mike darted his eyes, cupped a hand, and leaned in. "Gazpacho," he whispered.

"What's Gazpacho?" Grego asked.

"A snake-headed dragon with scissors for hands," said Dino Mike.

Ash sank her claws into Betty's rib cage. "Ow," Betty said. "Quit playing, Michael. You're scaring the kids."

The sun poked its head into view, spiking the temperature ten degrees. "All right," Shank said, mopping his brow. He pointed to the second biggest mushroom. "Randy, you guys take that one. Michael, you and the raptors crash here."

"Here" happened to be the smallest rock by a wide margin. Meanwhile, Shank and Betty carried Ash and Fern to the largest. Delilah followed.

"Where are you going?" Shank said.

"I'm coming with you," said Delilah.

"I don't think there's enough room," said Shank. "I just want to make sure Betty can get some sleep knowing the girls are safe. Why don't you bunk with Michael and them?"

*Clack-clack. Clack-clack. Clack-cla—*

Shrapnel stopped banging his coconuts. His eyes fell on a jagged boulder at the base of the canopy.

*Thwack! Thwack! Thwack!*

Shrapnel bashed his coconuts against the rock. Still, they failed to crack open. Fed up, Hack snatched the coconuts and launched them like Nerf balls into oblivion. One took the arm clean off a cactus. Bernadette smiled, enjoying the peace.

"Hey," Shrapnel said. "There's milk in those."

Dino Mike shook his head and scanned the ground. A twig jutted out. He dug around the base, yanked out a bulbous root, and popped a squat in the shade. He filed root shavings into a pile. Delilah cleared her throat.

"What are you doing here?" Dino Mike said.

"I don't like Troodons, and I can't stand Shank," said Delilah. "I'm crashing here. If you have a problem with that, you can sleep somewhere else."

"Whatever," Dino Mike said. "Make yourself comfortable. Just leave me alone."

"Fine," Delilah said. "Don't call me ugly again, and maybe I will."

"Fine."

"Fine." Delilah sat adjacent to Dino Mike and crossed her arms.

Shrapnel snooped around in search of his coconuts. The severed cactus arm caught his eye. He prodded it with his spear.

"Guys," Shrapnel said. "Guys."

Bernadette and Hack rolled their eyes. "What is it?" Bernie said.

"There's milk in here," said Shrapnel. He held the skewered cactus chunk up.

"What are they doing?" Delilah said.

Dino Mike glanced over. Shrapnel tilted back his head. "I wouldn't do that if I was you," said Dino Mike.

"Why not?" said Shrapnel.

"Cactus water is non-potable," said Dino Mike.

"I don't care if it's potato or not-potato," said Shrapnel. "It's wet." He poured. A frothy string of off-white foam oozed onto his tongue.

"Suit yourself," Dino Mike said. He whittled his root, minding his own business.

"I want some," Delilah said. She stood, and Dino Mike grabbed her.

"Don't," said Dino Mike. Delilah knocked him away. Dino Mike shrugged. "Fine. Do. It will make you sick, is all. Fair warning."

Delilah watched Hack and Bernie struggle with hunks of ruptured cactus. "Are they going to get sick?"

"Yep."

"Why aren't you stopping them?"

"What else can I do?" Dino Mike said. "Plus, they burned down our den. They deserve what's coming."

"And we're supposed to die of thirst?" Delilah asked.

"Of course not," said Dino Mike. He packed a ball of root shavings and passed it to Delilah. "There's water in the desert if you know where to look."

"What do I do with this?" Delilah said.

"Squeeze it as hard as you can," said Dino Mike. He packed another ball up and stood. "Or don't. That's up to you."

"Where are you going?" said Delilah.

"To give Ash and Fern a drink."

\* \* \*

The following night was even colder and darker. The Troodon children shivered in shadowy lumps under Trina's feathers. Randy reached out and touched his own breath.

Delilah squeezed a root ball over her mouth. She wiped her jaw and flashed Dino Mike a meager smile, a small token of her appreciation. Dino Mike barely smiled back.

Something croaked at the back of the pack. Shrapnel grimaced and grabbed his gut.

"Was that you?" Hack said.

"Actually, it might have been me," said Bernadette. She hunched, and her abdomen whinnied.

"What's wrong with—" Hack started, but his belly bubbled, and he doubled over. "Oh," he said. "Shank. Shank, we have to stop for a—oh!"

Shank turned around. The raptors dipped behind three Joshua trees. Irregular noises ensued. Delilah giggled. Dino Mike smirked.

"What's with them?" Shank asked.

"Who knows?" said Dino Mike.

Betty shivered and nuzzled Ash. Fern's sleepy head popped out from under Shank's feathers.

"How much farther is it, Michael?" Betty said.

"Seriously," said Shank. "The girls are freezing." He caressed Fern's crown, tightening Dino Mike's nerves like strings.

Dino Mike fought his acid reflux and climbed a rocky dune. He surveyed the desert and spotted a speck of orange light flickering in the distance.

"What's that?" Shank said. The light went out.

"What's what?" said Dino Mike.

"I thought I saw something," said Shank. "I don't see it now."

"I didn't see anything," said Dino Mike. "The boneyard's only another few miles. Do you want to wait for the raptors or not?"

* * *

Dino Mike tiptoed over a spinal column where the vertebrae met the skull. Shank's foot came down from the top, crushing the skull to chalky bits.

The Troodons and deinonychuses formed a circle around Gazpacho's firepit. Two Y-shaped sticks stood like divining rods, but the spit was nowhere to be found.

"What's that?" Randy asked.

"A fireplace," said Dino Mike. "I can light it if you're cold."

"No fires," said Shank. "You've burned down enough."

"Rocks don't burn," Dino Mike said. "They keep the fire from spreading."

Shank scraped dirt from under his claw. "You better keep the fire from starting."

"He's right, Michael," Betty said. "You remember what happened last time. The sun will be up soon enough. We can keep each other warm until then."

Delilah threw up in her mouth.

"Where can we sleep?" Shank said.

Dino Mike pointed. "Master suite's over there. Second rib cage on the left."

"Show us," said Shank.

"But of course," said Dino Mike.

Groober's poncho lay on the floor of the rib cage. Dino Mike scooped it up and wrapped Ash and Betty. Shank peeled a palm leaf from the wall. Tar stuck to his feathers.

"The Herbies did that," Dino Mike said. "It blocks out the wind and the sun."

Betty reached for Fern. Shank took a step back.

"Give her to me," Betty said. Reluctantly, Shank forfeited his leverage.

"Stay here," Shank said. "Michael and I need to have a word."

Dino Mike followed Shank outside.

"I hope you're not thinking about trying anything stupid," Shank said.

"Have we met?" said Dino Mike. "I'll die before I let you hurt her."

"You don't have any say in the matter," said Shank. "Keep doing what you're doing, and everything will be fine."

"How do I know that?"

Shank grinned. "I want to see the rest of this map. No tricks."

Dino Mike snatched Shank's spear. Shank growled. Dino Mike held up a frail arm.

"Chill," Dino Mike said. He glanced up and drew a map in the dirt with Poseidon facing north. "You see those stars? Right now, they're facing up. If we turn left, they face right, which is the way to the water tree."

"What's this on the other side?" Shank asked.

"Tar pits," Dino Mike said. "I don't know what you know about those, but tar pits and dinosaurs don't mix."

Flashing light cut the conversation short. Dino Mike and Shank rushed to investigate. The Troodons and raptors, who had finally caught up, surrounded the firepit. The raptors were sweaty messes.

"What is this?" Shank demanded.

"It's a fire," Randy said. "It's warm."

"I understand," said Shank. "Who lit it?"

Nobody answered, but Bernadette grinned. Shank scooped up a handful of dirt. Randy stepped in front of him.

"We're freezing, Shank," Randy said. "We'll put it out when the sun comes up."

Betty walked up behind them. "It is warm," she added. "And it does look safe. Maybe it's not such a big deal."

Shank scowled and threw the dirt to the ground.

\* \* \*

The Carnies sat in a ring around the campfire, soaking in its warmth. Randy took a swig from a root ball and passed it to Grego. Bernadette swiped another from Hack, used it to quenched her own thirst, and flipped the remains to Shrapnel. Shrapnel squeezed. It was bone-dry.

Fern hopped over a humerus and scootched past a set of narrow phalanges. Someone picked her up from behind.

"Where do you think you're going?" Delilah said. She took a seat by the fire and set Fern in her lap. "It's not safe to wander off."

Ash, who was finally awake, let go of Betty's hip and crawled over to join her sister. Betty smiled warmly and wrapped herself in the blanket. Delilah's eyes returned the goodwill.

"Does anybody know a good story?" Delilah asked.

"I do," Dino Mike said. "It's a tale about the dagger-wielding demon who's probably sharpening his knives and watching us right now."

Ash burrowed under Delilah's feathers. Fern rolled her eyes.

"Michael, stop it," Betty said. "We talked about this."

"Fine," said Dino Mike. "At least you can't say I didn't warn you."

The fire popped like corn. Grego stirred in his seat. "Yo, is this place really haunted though?" Grego asked.

"It is," Dino Mike said. "But you probably don't have anything to worry about. Gazpacho prefers women and children, mothers especially. He'll be full long before he gets to you."

"I'm serious, Michael," Betty said. She stood, and the blanket fell. "I'm not going to tell you again."

Dino Mike stoked the fire. A gust of wind blew it out. Grego screamed.

"What was that?" Hack said. Something rustled like leaves, and creepy, woodwind music played out of nowhere. "Light that fire back up!"

"I'm trying," Bernadette said. She strummed two sticks together. Finally, they sparked. "Got it."

The Carnies scanned the premises. Grego let go of Randy. Trina did not let go of her kids. Shank and Betty exchanged glances. Delilah, Ash, and Fern were gone.

"Where are the girls?" Betty exclaimed.

Dino Mike ripped a strip of fur from the blanket and wrapped it around a bone. He dunked it in tar and lit a torch. Shank snatched it, and the campfire blew out again. Grego screamed some more.

"What's going on?" Randy said. He copied Dino Mike by dunking a blanket-wrapped bone in the tar. He touched the tip of it to Shank's and lit a torch of his own. He waved it around, but Trina and her children were nowhere to be found. "Trina?"

An ominous xylobone chilled the Carnies' spines. They backed into a huddle. Shadows danced like puppets around them.

"Where are my girls?" Betty repeated.

"What's that?" Grego said. He pushed Randy's forearm, illuminating a rib cage. Gazpacho's hand wrapped around the edge of it like an eight-legged freak. Randy went pale, and his torch blew out.

"Look out!" Shank yelled.

The Carnies turned. Smoke billowed. Gazpacho limped out of the darkness and rubbed his scissors together, honing the blades. He flitted his tongue.

"Run!" Dino Mike said.

Gazpacho pounced. Dino Mike tripped over a leg bone and screamed.

"This way," Shank said, waving his torch westward.

Gazpacho slashed and snipped Dino Mike's feathers. Randy, Grego, and the raptors ran.

Betty hyperventilated, her face dripping with tears. Gazpacho snapped his snakehead around and shrieked like a banshee. Betty flashed her teeth, stepped forward, and whipped out her claws. A strong set of arms reeled Betty in from behind.

"He's gone," Shank said. "We have to go."

"I'm not leaving without my girls," said Betty.

"They're gone too," said Shank. "Like we will be if we don't leave now."

Betty's soul escaped her body, and her empty shell went rigid. Shank squatted, threw her over his shoulder, and booked it toward the flickering, orange speck in the distance.

"That went well," Gazpacho said.

"That went terrible," said Dino Mike. He sat up, sporting an edgy, new hairstyle. "Why didn't you get Betty?"

"I thought I did," said Gazpacho. He turned Dino Mike's head. "Now that's what I'm talking about. You look absolutely ferocious."

Dino Mike shoved him. "The one that wanted to fight you. That was Betty."

"Oh," said Gazpacho. "My bad. Who did I get?"

Inside the rib cage, Dino Mike untied Delilah's mouth and cut her hands free. She elbowed him, and he moved on to the miniature restraints binding Ash and Fern. Trina yelled, but it was muffled.

"I'm sorry," Dino Mike said. He cut her free too. She smacked him, hissed, and flicked out her claws. "Relax," said Dino Mike. "I'm saving your life. Gazpacho, do you have anything they can eat?"

"I have some hearts of palm and yuca left over from dinner," Gazpacho said.

"They can't eat that," said Dino Mike.

"Why not? It's cooked," said Gazpacho. He towered over Delilah, Trina, and the kids. They cowered in fear. "Don't be scared," Gazpacho said. He laid the grilled veggies at their feet. "There should be enough for everyone to get a bite."

Fern sniffed and pounced. She devoured a palm heart whole and burped. Dino Mike, Delilah, and Trina were floored.

"Do you mean to tell me we could have been eating plants all along?" Delilah said.

"Yeah," said Gazpacho. "But only if you cook them first."

"All plants?" said Dino Mike. "Not just olives?"

"I've been trying to tell you," said Gazpacho. "You should try listening when someone else is speaking."

Delilah and Trina dug in. "Mmm," Trina said. "This is heavenly."

Dino Mike stood at the door.

"What's up?" Gazpacho asked. "You don't want any?"

"I have to go," Dino Mike said.

"After your sister?"

"No. If Shank doesn't figure out I sent him the wrong way before he reaches the tar pits, he will when they do. He'll be back, and no amount of grilled veggies is going to stop him. I have to warn the Herbies."

"I see," Gazpacho said. He grimaced.

"What's wrong?" Dino Mike said. "You don't look so good, bud."

"Speak for yourself," said Gazpacho. "You look like a hand-me-down feather duster."

Dino Mike checked Gazpacho's leg. The wound was scabbed over with tricolored gunk.

"Ew. Your leg's getting worse," Dino Mike said. "We need to take care of that."

"What do you have in mind?" Gazpacho said.

"I have to get Harmonica to look at it. If the Herbies don't kill me, that is. Do you think you can keep my friends safe until the others get back?"

"They look pretty tough. Can you see if they'll watch after me?"

Delilah stood. "I want to go with you," she said.

"No way," said Dino Mike. "It's a one-way ticket. I probably won't make it back."

"I don't care," said Delilah. "I violated your trust, and I'd like to have that back. I'm coming along whether you like it or not."

"Is there anything I can do to change your mind?" Dino Mike asked.

"Not a chance," said Delilah. "Trina, can you watch the girls for Betty?"

"Of course," Trina said. "But what are you going to do when the sun comes up?"

"I don't know," said Delilah. "Try to find some shade, I guess?"

"There isn't any to be found," Dino Mike said. "There's a burnt Joshua tree patch a little more than halfway there. If we find that before the stars fade, we might be able to straight-line it the rest of the way. But the sun is going to blister us."

"If you can't find shade, why don't you take some with you?" Gazpacho said.

"How do we do that?" said Dino Mike.

Gazpacho cracked a rib from the side of the cage and held it up. Its palm leaves drooped like an umbrella.

"That could work," Dino Mike said. "Do you think we could get one more of those?"

Gazpacho cracked another rib. Dino Mike passed the first parasol to Delilah.

CHAPTER EIGHTEEN
# THE FIRE TREE

A glowing ember turned to charcoal. Shank Nightcuss curled his lip, and his torch fizzled out in the early morning twilight. A simmering tar bubble popped in an oleaginous pit.

"What's that?" Shrapnel asked.

"What's it look like?" said Hack. "It's what you have for brains."

Shrapnel elbowed Hack. Hack poked back. Shrapnel gave Hack a wallop. Hack wound up and threw a haymaker, but he missed and knocked Bernadette into a teepee. It collapsed in a heap of skin and bone.

Bernadette sat up with a fibula. Mammal fur drooped from the end of it, dousing her in shade. Bernadette gritted her teeth. Hack's color turned to ash like the torch.

"She's going to kill you," Shrapnel said.

Randy dunked his hand in the pit and held up a claw. Tar dribbled like molasses.

"How did this happen?" Randy said.

"He tricked us," said Shank. "North doesn't change. He sent us here on purpose."

"Why would he do that?" said Betty. Her eyes were wrinkled, and her feathers were frayed. "Did you see what that thing did to him? To all of them? My girls? This is all your fault."

Betty lashed out with a fist. Shank's eyeballs bulged.

"Look out!" Shank yelled. He caught Betty's wrist and chucked her aside. The ground trembled. The Carnies gasped. A slashed-up allosaurus pawed the ground and snorted. Shank, Randy, and Grego unhinged their claws. The allosaurus roared.

\* \* \*

A solar flare sliced through the water tree's branches. A single pearl of sweat slipped down Groober Spinx's tusk. Groober meditated at the top of the trench. The pipes Penny and Anna had been able to remove were stacked behind him in haphazard piles.

"We're running out of time," Penny said. "Why don't we just flush out the rest?"

"The ground is too permeable," said Groober. "It'll soak the water up. That's why we piped it to the riverbed in the first place."

"Let's stomp them out, then," said Penny. "Every last one of them."

"That's a terrible idea," Groober said. "I don't know what else to say."

Anna chuckled against the pump with one hoof in a strap. A pair of palm trees glided toward them in the distance, making her raise her eyebrows.

"Uh, Groober?"

"Let me guess. You have an idea too?"

"No," Anna said. "Look, dummy."

Groober and Penny turned. The palm trees glided closer.

"Michael Deinonychus, you fopdoodle," Groober said. Penny cracked her knuckles and balled up her fists.

Dino Mike marched with Delilah. She was dingy and covered in dirt.

"This isn't going to go well," Dino Mike said. "You better let me do the talking."

Delilah nodded. They lowered their umbrellas. Anna, Groober, and Penny formed a perimeter around them. Penny twirled a shovel.

"Dino Mike," Anna said. "Welcome back."

"Hello, Anna," Dino Mike said. "Penny. Mr. Spinx."

"Who's the babe?" Anna asked.

"This is Delilah," said Dino Mike. "Don't worry. She's a friend."

"She's cute," said Anna.

Delilah leaned in toward Dino Mike's ear. "I thought you said this wasn't going to go well?"

Groober cleared his throat. "What are you doing here?"

"We have orders to kill you on sight," Penny said.

"I've got this, Penny," said Groober. "We, uh, have orders to kill you on sight." Penny cracked her neck.

"We came here fully knowing that," Dino Mike said. "But you can't. You need us."

"Psh. For what?" said Groober.

"There's a storm coming," Dino Mike said. "This one's worse than the last one."

\* \* \*

With the blade of an axe, Brute Grimstone scalped the top from a tree. Around him, dozens of felled palms were stacked in untidy piles. The repurposed beams from Harvey's unfinished wall were among them.

*Ka-chunk!*

Taddle Bill yanked his axe by the handle, but it wouldn't budge from his tree's pineapple-like bark. Harvey roved over and gave the axe a tug. It popped free, and he blew like he was snuffing a candle. The tree toppled over.

"Timber," Harvey said. "Do me a favor and make sure it makes its way to a pile."

Taddle scowled at Harvey like he was a plateful of olives.

Harmonica pinned Sonny down. "Hold still," she said. Sonny struggled. Harmonica slathered his nose with slimy, green herbs.

"Gross. It smells," Sonny said.

"I don't care," said Harmonica. "You need protection from the sun."

Harvey strolled up behind them. Harmonica sniffed and scrunched up her nose.

"Uck. What do you want?" Harmonica said.

Harvey scratched his dome. "How'd you know it was me?"

"Lucky guess," said Harmonica. "Sonny, why don't you go check on Eggbert?"

Sonny mean-mugged Harvey and ran off. Harmonica kept her back to him.

"Why the long face?" Harvey said. "Aren't you getting what you wanted?"

"Indentured servitude wasn't part of the deal," said Harmonica.

"You don't have to carry any pipes if you don't want to," Harvey said. "Anyone else who wants to go back to the Good Lands has to pay their way out. Sweat equity."

Harmonica surveyed the herd of lumberjacks. They might as well have been prisoners.

"Who doesn't want to go?" Harmonica said.

Harvey smiled. "You could never see the jungle for the trees. Let Granny know we're on schedule for tonight."

\* \* \*

The allosaurus whinnied and flailed its tiny arms. It was up to its chest in tar.

"What do you want to do about that?" Randy inquired.

"I think we can use him," Shank said.

"Come again?" said Randy.

Shank hardened his gaze. The allosaurus's eyes softened. "He looks hungry, doesn't he?" Shank said. "Go on, throw the dinosaur some rope."

Randy gulped and looked to Grego. The allosaurus neighed. Grego jumped.

\* \* \*

Dino Mike coughed out a mouthful of chalk. He and Delilah were bound back-to-back at the shoulders and knees. The world was on its side.

"What do you see?" Delilah asked.

Anna, Groober, and Penny argued in a huddle.

"Nothing auspicious," said Dino Mike.

"What makes you think he was lying?" Anna said.

"He opened his mouth," said Penny.

"What happens on the off chance he's telling the truth?" Anna asked. "What if there really are twelve packs of Carnies coming this way?"

"All the more reason to kill them now," said Penny. "Two fewer enemies to deal with."

"C'mon, Groober," Anna said. "You know what you did to him was wrong. Help a Carnie out."

"I don't know," said Groober. "Maybe we should wait for Harvey on this."

"What would Harvey do?" Penny demanded.

"Put his head on a stick, probably," said Groober. "But he might want to gather more information first."

"We can't wait for him here," Dino Mike urged. "There's no time. We have to go now."

"We can't leave," Groober said. "If we don't destroy these termites, there won't be a Great Lands to go to."

"Why didn't you say so?" said Delilah.

"Come again?" said Groober.

"Look at who you're talking to," Delilah said. "If there's one thing Michael Deinonychus excels at, it's destruction. I've seen him burn down entire dens."

Groober grew an inch. "Why didn't I think of that?"

"Think of what?" said Delilah.

"Penny, Anna, get those logs back in the trench," said Groober.

"What for?" Anna said.

Groober snapped a stick in half. "We're going to light these suckers up."

"All right," Anna said. She squatted and stretched her arms. "But only because I haven't worked out yet today."

"A fire," Dino Mike muttered. "Of course." He glanced at the water tree.

"Agh!" Delilah yelled. Penny hoisted Delilah and Dino Mike over her head.

"Penny, what are you doing?" Groober asked.

"We're not taking any chances," Penny said. "These two can burn with the bugs."

With a clang, Penny had her bell rung, and her kneecaps buckled. Dino Mike and Delilah fell to the ground. Penny turned around. Anna gasped and hid Penny's shovel behind her back. Penny reached for Anna's throat, but her eyes rolled, and her body tipped over. Groober was stupefied.

"What?" Anna said with a shrug. "Were you really going to let her go and do all that?" She dropped the shovel and knelt to loosen Dino Mike's ropes. Dino Mike hopped to his feet.

"Thanks, Anna," Dino Mike said.

"No sweat, toots." She went to work untying Delilah.

"Groober," Dino Mike said. "We're out of time. Forget about the Great Lands and the termites. They'll mean nothing if you're dead. We need to get a signal to Harvey."

Groober scoffed and crossed his arms. Delilah joined Anna at Dino Mike's side, nullifying Groober's vote.

"What did you have in mind?" Groober asked.

"Remember the Joshua trees?" Dino Mike said.

Groober looked over Dino Mike's shoulder. The water tree's bark peeled in the wind.

"Oh no," Groober said. He waved his hands. "No, no, no, no, no. Absolutely not. Zero chance. One hundred percent, no way."

\* \* \*

"Harvey!" Brute said. Harvey didn't respond. His head lay back, and he snored loudly atop a stack of sawed logs. Brute nudged Taddle. "Wake him up."

Taddle shook Harvey's elbow. A log rolled out, and Harvey conked his head on the one beneath it. "Harvey," Taddle said. "It's an emergency. Look."

In the distance, charcoal-black smoke twisted like an apocalyptic tornado.

"Who knows how to start a fire?" Brute said.

"Sound the alarm," said Harvey. He snarled and shattered half the logs with a swipe of his tail.

\* \* \*

In the giant rib cage, the Troodon children fanned Ash and Fern with palm leaves. Trina napped. Gazpacho bit the tip off a flame-kissed yuca root. The ground tremored rhythmically, and the young Troodons dropped their fans. Trina sat up and looked at the door.

"What was that?" Trina asked.

Gazpacho unfurled his claws. "Stay here."

Gazpacho slid along the skeletons outside and surveyed the sunburnt yard. The tremors grew nearer, and he dove behind a rock. Shank Nightcuss and the Carnies marched past unfettered. Randy and Grego steered the muzzled allosaurus with king-size bamboo leashes. Bernadette, Hack, and Shrapnel shaded Betty and Shank with mammal-skin screens.

## CHAPTER NINETEEN
# THE FEAST

Harvey Plates swung his battle-axe at his side, hocked a loogie, and spat. A panicked dung beetle dove behind a dusty ball of poop. The phlegm bomb detonated. A small exodus of Herbies paraded up the riverbank.

Granny Pacquiao puckered atop Brute Grimstone's shoulders. Sunblock was smeared on the top of her crown and the tip of her snout. Taddle, Norm, and the other iguanodons were glued to Harvey's hips. Harmonica and Miranda formed a contingent of their own off to the side. Nobody said a word.

The ozone reeked of ashtray. Smoke dispersed into ether. The Herbies formed a crescent on the east side of the trench. Miranda pushed her way through the ruck. The pressure pump nodded in full working order. Across the trench, the supply tents swayed in the breeze. As for the water tree and every pipe in the line, they were burned to crispy smithereens.

Anna, Groober, Dino Mike, and Delilah emerged from the tents and lined up along the trench's western edge. Granny snorted. Brute smirked. Miranda's arteries constricted. Harvey's knuckles turned white, and his grip splintered his axe handle. Harmonica had trouble breathing. Her cheeks felt like they were on fire, and her heart sank like it was made of lead.

"Harvey," Anna said. "It is so good to see you. Grandmother, Harmonica, you look nice."

Granny patted Brute's tricep. "Put me down," she said. Brute knelt, and she clonked his head. "Not here, numbskull. I can't hear what they're saying. Put me down over there."

"Where's Penny?" Harvey asked.

"She's in the tent," Dino Mike said. "Restrained, but unharmed. She was being . . . aggressive."

"Of course she was," said Harvey. He punched a hole in the dirt with his tail. "Her orders were to kill any Carnies on sight."

Granny slid down Brute's neck and, with her walking stick, wobbled up to the trench.

"Grandmother," Dino Mike said.

"I'm not your grandma. Now, do you want to tell me what the dung is going on?" Dino Mike curled his lip. Granny pointed her stick at him. "You shut your mouth before you speak to me," Granny said. "I want the truth. Every bit of it. If you're thinking about lying, you'd better think about how slowly and painfully I can end you."

Dino Mike dreaded the thought.

"C'mon, then," said Granny. "Before I turn gray."

Dino Mike cleared his throat. "The Carnies are coming," he said.

"I beg your pardon?" said Granny.

"The Carnies are coming," Mike repeated. "I tried to stop them, but I couldn't. I sent them to the tar pits first to buy us some time, but they must've figured that out by now."

Granny knuckled her eyepatch. "How do they know we are here?"

"Because of me," Dino Mike said. "I drew them a map."

"How could you?" said Harmonica. She shoved Harvey aside. "After we took you in and cared for you, knowing full and darn well how dangerous it was? Shame on you."

"It wasn't that simple, Harmonica," said Dino Mike. "I didn't have a choice."

"Don't feed me that slop," said Harmonica. "You always have a choice."

"Excuse me, hello?" Delilah said. "I don't know who you are, but I don't think you understand. If Michael didn't give Shank, my ex-boyfriend who recently killed his own brother, aka Michael's sister Betty's husband Odin, the map, Shank was going to murder his niece. He had to do it. He did *not* have a choice."

"How many are there?" Granny said.

"I don't know for certain," said Dino Mike. "It could be anywhere from five to fourteen."

"That doesn't sound like twelve packs to me," Anna muttered.

"Eh?" said Granny.

"Nothing," said Anna. She smiled. "Carry on."

Groober bit his tusk.

"There's a chance we can stop them before they attack," Dino Mike said. "We'd have to team up, but if it works, nobody has to get hurt."

"What do you mean 'we'?" said Harvey.

"He means us," said Delilah. "All of us."

"And who are you?" Harvey said. "Other than the Carnie who burned down my tree?"

"The one who took care of your termite problem and kept your pump and irrigation thingies intact," said Delilah. "Which, by the way, you're welcome. We didn't have to do that."

"I think what Delilah is trying to say is we came here to help," Dino Mike added.

"How noble of you," said Harmonica. "Considering this is all your fault to begin with."

"That is not untrue," Groober said. "But it doesn't make us need him any less."

"You think we should trust him?" said Harmonica.

"Of course not," said Groober. "Dino Mike toasted that bridge like he has every other significant landmark in his life. He's not to be trusted. But he's right about one thing. We may be able to avoid bloodshed."

"Expound," said Granny.

"This is a working theory, but when Contessa seasons her olives, she does it on a rock that lies directly in the sun," Groober said. "That rock absorbs enough energy to lightly cook the olives, which makes them susceptible to the Carnies' digestive enzymes. I think. At any rate, they can eat them."

"McBeek," Granny said.

"Yes, Grandmother?" said Miranda.

"What is this foolio blabbing about?"

"I think he's implying that Carnies are able to consume olives, but only if they are heated to a certain minimum internal temperature first," Miranda said.

"Not just olives," Groober said. "Vegetables. And we've streamlined the process by adding controlled fire to the equation."

"Bull hockey," said Harvey. "You can't be serious."

Anna tossed a skewer of olives over the trench. It landed at Harvey's and Granny's feet. "He's serious," Anna said. "And bulls don't play hockey."

Harvey picked up the skewer, and his stomach sang an opera. He bit the stick in half.

"Mmm. It's good."

"See?" Dino Mike said.

Granny clapped. "That's lovely. Bravo. But what happens when your Carnies eat that and wonder what a grilled Herbie tastes like?"

Harvey licked his teeth. Delilah's tummy grumbled. She smiled nervously.

"I hope that doesn't happen," Dino Mike said. "But it might, so we have to be prepared."

"How do you propose we do that?" Harmonica asked. "Do you have a plan?"

Dino Mike framed the trench with his fingers and shrugged. "I don't know. Part of one, maybe. I wouldn't be Dino Mike if I didn't."

\* \* \*

Shank Nightcuss's claws clinked like spurs. His shadow appeared at the top of a rocky dune. Shank looked askance at the ashes and Herbies on the horizon. The corners of his eyes were covered in wrinkles.

Penny, Taddle, Brute, Anna, Delilah, Harmonica, Miranda, Norm, and the iguanodons locked elbows like picketers beyond the pressure pump. They were covered head to hoof in mud. Harvey, Granny, Dino Mike, and Groober stood in solidarity fifty yards away. There was no trench between them.

"They're here," Dino Mike said.

"Where?" said Groober.

"Up there," said Dino Mike. "On the left."

Groober looked to his right. He saw nothing but dirt.

On the back side of the dune, the hangry allosaurus heaved at its cables. Randy, Grego, and the raptors hoed to hold him back. Betty's shadow appeared next to Shank's.

"Is that Michael?" Betty said. "And Delilah? What's going on?"

"Wait, what?" Randy said. He let go of his rope. Grego and the raptors lurched but recovered. It took all of their weight to restrain the allosaurus. Randy joined Shank and Betty atop the dune. "Is Trina there too?"

"I don't see her," said Betty.

"We need to find out," said Randy. "Like now."

Shank lifted his spear. "Keep the big guy out of sight," he said. "Wait for my signal."

Against the blue sky, a bare-boned vulture glided on frail wings. Beneath it, Shank, Betty, and Randy closed the gap between them and their waiting audience.

"Betty," Dino Mike said. "I am so sorry."

"How are you alive?" Betty said. "And what happened to my babies?"

"They're safe," said Mike. "I left them in the boneyard with Trina and Gazpacho. The Troodon kids too."

"Gazpacho?" Betty said.

"Sí, Gazpacho," said Dino Mike. "My amigo. You met him the other night." Betty opened her mouth, but Dino Mike cut her off. "Before you ask any more questions, just know Shank threatened to hurt Fern. I did what I had to do to protect her."

"That's a lie," Shank said.

Betty ignored him. "What are you doing here?"

"Negotiating peace," Dino Mike said. "And protecting my friends." He extended a literal olive branch. It was caramelized and had a nice char.

"Are you still going on about those?" Betty asked.

"I know you can smell them," said Dino Mike. "Please, just give them a try. This one came straight off the grill."

Betty hesitated.

"Go on," Granny Pacquiao said. "What have you got to lose?" Reluctantly, Betty took the branch and nibbled the fruit.

"Wow," Betty said. "That is delicious."

The scent punched Randy in the nose and made his mouth water. "Can I try?" he said. Betty passed him the branch. Randy took a bite. "Mmm. Mm-hm. Shank, you got to try this."

Shank growled lowly. Randy handed him the olives. Dino Mike gritted his teeth. Shank tightened the grip on his spear. Harvey squeezed his axe.

"I didn't come here to eat vegetables," Shank said. He threw the olives on the ground and stomped on them like they were Dino Mike's heart. "How's this going to go? Are we going to have an all-out rumble? Or would you rather we play things slow and pick you off one by one?"

"I have an idea," Granny said. "Let's settle this the old-fashioned way. My best against your best. One versus one."

"I'm game," said Shank. "Who's it going to be, Grandma? You versus me?"

Harvey rolled his shoulders. "You wish."

"It should be me," Dino Mike said.

"No way," said Harvey. "I'll mash this chump like pesto."

"No, really," said Dino Mike. "It was my plan that failed. And it's my fault we're in this mess. Plus, no one else knows Shank like I do. It has to be me."

"I agree," Granny said. "Step down, Harvey. Dino Mike will be my champion."

"Dino Mike?" Betty said.

"Sí," said Granny. "Di-no Mike."

"Challenge accepted," Shank said. He twirled his spear like a baton.

"Don't be ridiculous," said Betty. "What are you agreeing to?"

"A fight to the death, of course," said Shank.

Betty flicked out her claws. "I said that's not happening. I won't let you fight my brother."

"Who said I was fighting him?" Shank said. He nodded, and Randy held Betty like a straitjacket. She flailed and kicked to no avail. Shank cocked his head and barked.

"What's happening?" Dino Mike said.

The ground shook. Groober Spinx looked up. The unmuzzled allosaurus roared.

"Oh, crud," Dino Mike said.

Groober went pale and passed out. Harvey dropped Corrine and threw Granny over his shoulder. They booked it south. Dino Mike tried to scoop the axe by the handle, but the head was too heavy, and it dragged in the dirt. The allosaurus reared and charged. Dino Mike ran for the line of Herbies.

"What do we do now?" Taddle said. Norm and the iguanodons took off. The rest of the Herbies tightened their elbows.

"Hold the line!" Anna yelled.

Dino Mike punctured his foot on a stray cactus prick and stumbled. The allosaurus clamped its jaws, blasting Mike from behind with rotten-meat breath. Dino Mike pumped his arms.

"Hold the line!" Dino Mike yelled.

The allosaurus closed in and grazed the tip of Dino Mike's tail with his teeth. Harmonica squeezed her eyes shut. Dino Mike took one last step and leapt. The allosaurus lunged, and the ground crumbled beneath him. Dino Mike landed on solid ground. The allosaurus slammed his head on the ledge and collapsed in the trench.

Dino Mike picked up a rock. Adrenaline coursed through his veins. The Herbies peered closer. Locked and loaded, Dino Mike looked in the trench. The allosaurus lay in slumber. Dino Mike tossed the rock aside. The Herbies hooted and cheered.

"Impossible," Shank said.

Betty butted Randy in the grill with the back of her head and shook free. "Everything my brother does is impossible."

Dino Mike crossed over the top of the trench in front of the pump and met Shank eye-to-eye. Shank growled and whirled his spear.

"Shank, no," Betty said. She grabbed him, but he whipped her to the ground. Dino Mike froze. Between them, Groober lifted his head in a daze. Shank held his spear like a javelin and charged.

"Groober, on your left!" Dino Mike yelled.

Groober looked left. Shank hopped, pulled his arm back, and aimed for Mike.

"Ah!" Groober yelled.

Dino Mike stood tall. Groober Spinx rolled over and stretched out. Shank went to launch his spear, but his foot came down on Groober's quills, and the weapon sailed into the dirt. Shank hobbled and twisted in pain. Odin's claw swung loosely around his neck. Shank tumbled and crashed to the ground. Dino Mike and Betty ran over.

Dino Mike helped Groober sit up. Groober sputtered to gain his breath.

"Groober, you saved my life," Dino Mike said.

"Yeah, well, technically speaking, I owed you one," said Groober.

"How did you know which way to look?"

"Believe it or not, my lifetime average hovers around fifty percent."

Shank wheezed on the ground. Dino Mike helped Betty roll him over. The butt of Odin's claw stuck out of his chest. Shank gasped, knocked Dino Mike's hands away, and looked up at the sky. Two puffy clouds fought like brothers. Shank scoffed, and his muscles went lax.

Betty's eyes welled up. Dino Mike put his arm around her. Betty buried her head and let it all out. Across the trench, Delilah fell to her knees and broke down too. Anna was there to rub her shoulders.

Grego and the raptors came over and joined Randy. Something walking up the trench caught Randy's eye.

"Trina?" Randy said.

Dino Mike and Betty looked up. Harvey and Granny stood with Trina and all five Carnie children. Betty fell to her knees. Ash and Fern sprinted and leapt into her arms. Randy embraced Trina. Freckles and his twin hugged the runt.

Taddle Bill screamed. Panic charged the crowd like a bull. The allosaurus growled and lifted its head. Looking the Herbies over, it licked its teeth and roared.

"Hello, old friend," a voice said. The allosaurus turned. The Herbies all gasped.

"Gazpacho?" Dino Mike said.

Gazpacho fanned out his claws. His body was overwhelmed with with sepsis. "I'm your huckleberry."

"Are you all right?" Dino Mike asked.

Gazpacho hacked and dry-heaved. The wound on his leg bubbled, and he keeled over. The allosaurus grinned. Behind him, Brute Grimstone gulped.

Penny Plates's eyes fell on a shovel. She pushed Brute aside and stepped on the shovel's head, catapulting the handle up.

"Yah!" Penny yelled. She leapt from the top of the trench and patted her elbow in midair, bashing it against the allosaurus's neck. The allosaurus folded. Penny stood, swung the shovel over her head, and brought down the heat. The allosaurus's tail shot up and fell. Anna covered Brute's eyes.

"Gazpacho!" Dino Mike said. He placed an ear on Gazpacho's chest, but it barely registered a beat. "Harmonica! Harmonica, please. I need your help!"

Harmonica froze wide-eyed. Miranda jabbed her in the ribs.

"What should I do?" Harmonica asked.

"Go help him," Miranda said.

"Is it safe?" said Harmonica.

"He's undefeated against that allosaurus," Miranda said. "I think you'll be fine."

Harmonica trotted around the pressure pump while Delilah and Miranda watched her kneel next to Gazpacho and Dino Mike. Miranda smiled. Delilah sniffled and wiped her nose.

\* \* \*

Poseidon's teeth snapped the leaves from the top of a juicy palm. A medium-high tide rinsed white sand from the beach. Under a coconut tree, two rocks rested together in the shade.

Gazpacho's leg was wrapped in bandages, but his infection was mostly cleared up. Naturally, he shredded coleslaw in Contessa Treehorn's new kitchen. Contessa stoked the fire under her mammoth stone plancha. A gamut of trout and shellfish sizzled next to a spectrum of vegetables.

Shrapnel swung his leg back and kicked an apple-shaped stone. It bounced, skipped, and rolled within a few inches of another. Sonny Pacquiao smirked. He strolled over and hit his rock with a behind-the-back kick. It nicked Shrapnel's. Sonny lined up his toe and took seven or eight steps back. Shrapnel frowned.

Contessa sowed her grill top with exotic herbs and spices. A rock whizzed by and exploded over her head. Contessa flinched. A seafaring bird fell and landed on the grill. The rest of the bird's feathers fluttered down after it. Contessa glared down the beach. Dead to rights, Sonny pointed at Shrapnel.

"What was that?" Gazpacho said.

The smell of cooked bird snuck up to Contessa's nostrils. Contessa smiled pleasantly. "Never mind what that was," she said. She hit the bird with a dash of seasoning.

Contessa walked the roasted bird across the sand and presented it to Granny Pacquiao at the head of a table that ran the length of the beach. Every dinosaur in the Good Lands was present. Granny lifted her eyepatch and leaned in with her empty socket, pretending to get a better view.

"Looks good," Granny said. "Let's chow."

The dinosaurs whooped and pounded the table. Betty served Ash and Fern from a tray of charred prawns. Harmonica put a crispy brussels sprout stalk on Dino Mike's plate. Sonny stole another from Harmonica's platter. Dino Mike smiled and looked around the table. He hadn't taken a bite, but he already felt full. The Carnies and the Herbies shared a magnificent feast.

**Jason Singleton** is one rad dad. He loves watching football and eating cheeseburgers and dreams of doing snow angels on Mars.

Visit www.1TON.PRESS for more.